PENGU

SEVENTEENTH-CENTURY POETRY

SELECTED BY
PAUL DRIVER

PENGUIN BOOKS
A PENGUIN/GODFREY CAVE EDITION

PENGUIN BOOKS

Published by the Penguin Group
Penguin Books Ltd, 27 Wrights Lane, London w8 5tz, England
Penguin Books USA Inc., 375 Hudson Street, New York, New York 10014, USA
Penguin Books Australia Ltd, Ringwood, Victoria, Australia
Penguin Books Canada Ltd, 10 Alcorn Avenue, Toronto, Ontario, Canada m4v 3b2
Penguin Books (NZ) Ltd, 182–190 Wairau Road, Auckland 10, New Zealand

Penguin Books Ltd, Registered Offices: Harmondsworth, Middlesex, England

This edition first published 1995
Published in Penguin Popular Poetry 1996
1 3 5 7 9 10 8 6 4 2

Selection copyright © Paul Driver, 1995

Set in 9/10.5 pt Ehrhardt Monotype
Typeset by Datix International Limited, Bungay, Suffolk
Printed in England by Clays Ltd, St Ives plc

CONTENTS

The Pulley

When God at first made man,
Having a glass of blessings standing by,
Let us (said he) pour on him all we can:
Let the world's riches, which dispersèd lie,
        Contract into span.

So strength first made a way;
Then beauty flowed, then wisdom, honour, pleasure:
When almost all was out, God made a stay,
Perceiving that alone of all his treasure
        Rest in the bottom lay.

For if I should (said he)
Bestow this jewel also on my creature,
He would adore my gifts instead of me,
And rest in nature, not the God of nature:
        So both should losers be.

Yet let him keep the rest,
But keep them with repining restlessness:
Let him be rich and weary, that at least,
If goodness lead him not, yet weariness
        May toss him to my breast.

                              GEORGE HERBERT

'Love bade me welcome'

Love bade me welcome; yet my soul drew back,
        Guilty of dust and sin.
But quick-eyed love, observing me grow slack
        From my first entrance in,
Drew nearer to me, sweetly questioning
        If I lacked anything.

A guest, I answered, worthy to be here:
        Love said, 'You shall be he.'
I the unkind, ungrateful? 'Ah my dear,
        I cannot look on thee.'

Love took my hand, and smiling did reply,
>> 'Who made the eyes but I?'

'Truth Lord, but I have marred them: let my shame
>> Go where it doth deserve.'
'And know you not,' says love, 'who bore the blame?'
>> 'My dear, then I will serve.'
'You must sit down,' says love, 'and taste my meat':
>> So I did sit and eat.

GEORGE HERBERT

The Answer

My comforts drop and melt away like snow:
I shake my head, and all the thought and ends,
Which my fierce youth did bandy, fall and flow
Like leaves about me: or like summer friends,
Flies of estates and sunshine. But to all,
Who think me eager, hot, and undertaking,
But in my prosecutions slack and small;
As a young exhalation, newly waking,
Scorns his first bed of dirt, and means the sky;
But cooling by the way, grows pursy and slow,
And settling to a cloud, doth live and die
In that dark state of tears: to all, that so
>> Show me, and set me, I have one reply,
>> Which they that know the rest, know more than I.

GEORGE HERBERT

Colossians 3:3

>> Our life is hid with Christ in God.

My words and thoughts do both express this notion,
That Life hath with the sun a double motion.
The first Is straight, and our diurnal friend,
>> The other Hid and doth obliquely bend.
One life is wrapped In flesh, and tends to earth:
The other winds towards Him, whose happy birth
>> Taught me to live here so, That still one eye

Should aim and shoot at that which Is on high:
      Quitting with daily labour all My pleasure,
            To gain at harvest an eternal Treasure.

GEORGE HERBERT

A Song

Ask me no more where Jove bestows,
When June is past, the fading rose;
For in your beauty's orient deep
These flowers, as in their causes, sleep.

Ask me no more whither doth stray
The golden atoms of the day;
For in pure love heaven did prepare
Those powders to enrich your hair.

Ask me no more whither doth haste
The nightingale when May is past;
For in your sweet dividing throat
She winters and keeps warm her note.

Ask me no more where those stars light
The downwards fall in dead of night;
For in your eyes they sit, and there
Fixèd become, as in their sphere.

Ask me no more if east or west
The phoenix builds her spicy nest;
For unto you at last she flies,
And in your fragrant bosom dies.

THOMAS CAREW

The Good Morrow

I wonder by my troth, what thou and I
    Did, till we loved? Were we not weaned till then,
But sucked on country pleasures, childishly?
    Or snorted we in the seven sleepers' den?
'Twas so; but this, all pleasures fancies be.
If ever any beauty I did see,
Which I desired, and got, 'twas but a dream of thee.

3

And now good morrow to our waking souls,
    Which watch not one another out of fear;
For love, all love of other sights controls,
    And makes one little room, an every where.
Let sea-discovers to new worlds have gone,
Let maps to others, worlds on worlds have shown:
Let us possess one world, each hath one, and is one.

My face in thine eye, thine in mine appears,
    And true plain hearts do in the faces rest:
Where can we find two better hemispheres
    Without sharp north, without declining west?
Whatever dies, was not mixed equally;
If our two loves be one, or, thou and I
Love so alike that none do slacken, none can die.

JOHN DONNE

The Spring

Now that the winter's gone, the earth hath lost
Her snow-white robes, and now no more the frost
Candies the grass, or casts an icy cream
Upon the silver lake, or chrystal stream:
But the warm sunne thaws the benummed earth,
And makes it tender, gives a sacred birth
To the dead swallow; wakes in hollow tree
The drowsy cuckoo, and the humble-bee.
Now do a quire of chirping minstrels bring
In triumph to the world, the youthful spring.
The valleys, hills, and woods, in rich array,
Welcome the coming of the long'd-for May.
Now all things smile; only my Love doth lower:
Nor hath the scalding noon-day sunne the power,
To melt that marble ice, which still doth hold
Her heart congealed, and makes her pity cold.
The Ox which lately did for shelter fly
Into the stall, doth now securely lie
In open fields; and love no more is made
By the fire side; but in the cooler shade
Amyntas now doth with his Cloris sleep

Under a Sycamore, and all things keep
Time with the season, only she doth carry
June in her eyes, in her heart January.

THOMAS CAREW

On a Gentlewoman Walking in the Snow

I saw fair Cloris walk alone
Where feathered rain came softly down,
And Jove descended from his tower
To court her in a silver shower:
The wanton snow flew to her breast
Like little birds into their nest,
And overcome with whiteness there
For grief it thawed into a tear;
Thence falling on her garment's hem
For grief it freezed into a gem.

WILLIAM STRODE

The Canonization

For God's sake hold your tongue, and let me love;
  Or chide my palsy, or my gout,
My five grey hairs or ruined fortune flout,
With wealth your state, your mind with arts improve,
    Take you a course, get you a place,
    Observe his honour, or his grace,
Or the king's real, or his stampèd face
    Contémplate; what you will, approve,
      So you will let me love.

Alas, alas, who's injured by my love?
  What merchant's ships have my sighs drowned?
Who says my tears have overflowed his ground?
When did my colds a forward spring remove?
    When did the heats which my veins fill
    Add one more to the plaguy bill?
Soldiers find wars, and lawyers find out still
    Litigious men, which quarrels move,
      Though she and I do love.

Call us what you will, we're made such by love;
    Call her one, me another fly:
We're tapers too, and at our own cost die.
And we in us find the eagle and the dove;
        The phoenix riddle hath more wit
        By us: we two being one, are it;
So to one neutral thing both sexes fit.
        We die and rise the same, and prove
        Mysterious by this love.

We can die by it, if not live by love,
    And if unfit for tombs and hearse
Our legend be, it will be fit for verse;
And if no piece of chronicle we prove,
        We'll build in sonnets pretty rooms;
        As well a well wrought urn becomes
The greatest ashes, as half-acre tombs;
        And by these hymns, all shall approve
        Us canonized for love.

And thus invoke us: 'You whom reverend love
    Made one another's hermitage;
You, to whom love was peace, that now is rage;
Who did the whole world's soul contract, and drove
        Into the glasses of your eyes
        (So made such mirrors, and such spies,
That they did all to you epitomize)
        Countries, towns, courts: beg from above
        A pattern of your love!'

JOHN DONNE

The Dream

Dear love, for nothing less than thee
Would I have broke this happy dream,
        It was a theme
For reason, much too strong for phantasy,
Therefore thou waked'st me wisely; yet
My dream thou brok'st not, but continued'st it;

Thou art so true, that thoughts of thee suffice,
To make dreams truths, and fables histories;
Enter these arms, for since thou thought'st it best,
Not to dream all my dream, let's act the rest.

As lightning, or a taper's light,
Thine eyes, and not thy noise waked me;
        Yet I thought thee
(For thou lov'st truth) an angel, at first sight,
But when I saw thou saw'st my heart,
And knew'st my thought, beyond an angel's art,
When thou knew'st what I dreamed, when thou knew'st when
Excess of joy would wake me, and cam'st then,
I must confess, it could not choose but be
Profane, to think thee anything but thee.

Coming and staying showed thee, thee,
But rising makes me doubt, that now,
        Thou art not thou.
That love is weak, where fear's as strong as he;
'Tis not all spirit, pure, and brave,
If mixture it of fear, shame, honour, have.
Perchance as torches which must ready be,
Men light and put out, so thou deal'st with me,
Thou cam'st to kindle, goest to come; then I
Will dream that hope again, but else would die.

JOHN DONNE

Song

            Go, lovely rose!
        Tell her that wastes her time and me
            That now she knows,
        When I resemble her to thee,
        How sweet and fair she seems to be.

            Tell her that's young,
        And shuns to have her graces spied,
            That, hadst thou sprung
        In deserts where no men abide,
        Thou must have uncommended died.

Small is the worth
Of beauty from the light retired;
    Bid her come forth,
Suffer herself to be desired,
And not blush so to be admired.

    Then die; that she
The common fate of all things rare
    May read in thee:
How small a part of time they share
That are so wondrous sweet and fair!

EDMUND WALLER

Love's Growth

I scarce believe my love to be so pure
    As I had thought it was,
    Because it doth endure
Vicissitude, and season, as the grass;
Methinks I lied all winter, when I swore
My love was infinite, if spring make it more.
But if this medicine, love, which cures all sorrow
With more, not only be no quintessénce,
But mixed of all stuffs, paining soul, or sense,
And of the sun his working vigour borrow,
Love's not so pure and abstract as they use
To say, which have no mistress but their Muse,
But as all else, being elemented too,
Love sometimes would contémplate, sometimes do.

And yet not greater, but more eminent,
    Love by the spring is grown;
    As, in the firmament,
Stars by the sun are not enlarged, but shown,
Gentle love deeds, as blossoms on a bough,
From love's awakened root do bud out now.
If, as in water stirred more circles be
Produced by one, love such additions take,
Those like so many spheres, but one heaven make;
For, they are all concentric unto thee,
And though each spring do add to love new heat,

As princes do in times of action get
New taxes, and remit them not in peace,
No winter shall abate the spring's increase.

JOHN DONNE

A Nocturnal upon St Lucy's Day,
Being the Shortest Day

'Tis the year's midnight, and it is the day's,
Lucy's, who scarce seven hours herself unmasks;
   The sun is spent, and now his flasks
   Send forth light squibs, no constant rays;
     The world's whole sap is sunk:
The general balm th' hydroptic earth hath drunk,
Whither, as to the bed's-feet, life is shrunk,
Dead and interred; yet all these seem to laugh,
Compared with me, who am their epitaph.

Study me then, you who shall lovers be
At the next world, that is, at the next spring:
   For I am a very dead thing,
   In whom love wrought new alchemy.
     For his art did express
A quintessénce even from nothingness,
From dull privations, and lean emptiness:
He ruined me, and I am re-begot
Of absence, darkness, death; things which are not.

All others, from all things, draw all that's good,
Life, soul, form, spirit, whence they being have;
   I, by love's limbeck, am the grave
   Of all that's nothing. Oft a flood
     Have we two wept, and so
Drowned the whole world, us two; oft did we grow
To be two chaoses, when we did show
Care to aught else; and often absences
Withdrew our souls, and made us carcases.

But I am by her death (which word wrongs her)
Of the first nothing, the elixir grown;
   Were I a man, that I were one,

I needs must know; I should prefer,
    If I were any beast,
Some ends, some means; yea plants, yea stones detest,
And love; all, all some properties invest;
If I an ordinary nothing were,
As shadow, a light, and body must be here.

But I am none; nor will my sun renew.
You lovers, for whose sake the lesser sun
    At this time to the Goat is run
    To fetch new lust and give it you,
        Enjoy your summer all;
Since she enjoys her long night's festival,
Let me prepare towards her, and let me call
This hour her vigil, and her eve, since this
Both the year's, and the day's deep midnight is.

JOHN DONNE

The Vote

The helmet now an hive for bees becomes,
And hilts of swords may serve for spiders' looms;
        Sharp pikes may make
        Teeth for a rake;
And the keen blade, the arch-enemy of life,
Shall be degraded to a pruning knife;
        The rustic spade,
        Which first was made
For honest agriculture, shall retake
Its primitive employment, and forsake
        The rampires steep
        And trenches deep.
Tame conies in our brazen guns shall breed,
Or gentle doves their young ones there shall feed;
        In musket barrels
        Mice shall raise quarrels
For their quarters; the ventriloquious drum,
Like lawyers in vacations, shall be dumb;
        Now all recruits
        (But those of fruits)

Shall be forgot; and th'unarmed soldier
Shall only boast of what he did whilere,
    In chimneys' ends,
    Among his friends.
If good effects shall happy signs ensue,
I shall rejoice, and my prediction's true.

RALPH KNEVET

The Sun Rising

Busy old fool, unruly sun,
    Why dost thou thus
Through windows and through curtains call on us?
Must to thy motions lovers' seasons run?
    Saucy pedantic wretch, go chide
    Late schoolboys and sour prentices;
Go tell court huntsmen that the king will ride,
    Call country ants to harvest offices:
Love, all alike, no season knows, nor clime,
Nor hours, days, months, which are the rags of time.

    Thy beams, so reverend and strong
    Why shouldst thou think?
I could eclipse and cloud them with a wink,
But that I would not lose her sight so long:
    If her eyes have not blinded thine,
    Look, and tomorrow late tell me
Whether both th' Indias of spice and mine
Be where thou leftst them, or lie here with me.
Ask for those kings whom thou sawst yesterday,
And thou shalt hear, all here in one bed lay.

    She's all states, and all princes, I;
    Nothing else is.
Princes do but play us; compared to this,
All honour's mimic; all wealth alchemy.
    Thou, sun, art half as happy as we,
    In that the world's contracted thus;
Thine age asks ease, and since thy duties be
To warm the world, that's done in warming us.

Shine here to us, and thou art everywhere:
This bed thy centre is, these walls, thy sphere.

JOHN DONNE

Of the Last Verses in the Book

When we for age could neither read nor write,
The subject made us able to indite;
The soul, with nobler resolutions decked,
The body stooping, does herself erect.
No mortal parts are requisite to raise
Her that, unbodied, can her maker praise.
The seas are quiet when the winds give o'er;
So, calm are we when passions are no more!
For then we know how vain it was to boast
Of fleeting things, so certain to be lost.
Clouds of affection from our younger eyes
Conceal that emptiness which age descries.
The soul's dark cottage, battered and decayed,
Lets in new light through chinks that time has made
Stronger by weakness: wiser men become,
As they draw near to their eternal home;
Leaving the old, both worlds at once they view,
That stand upon the threshold of the new.

EDMUND WALLER

A Valediction: Forbidding Mourning

As virtuous men pass mildly away,
    And whisper to their souls to go,
Whilst some of their sad friends do say,
    The breath goes now, and some say, no:

So let us melt, and make no noise,
    No tear-floods, nor sigh-tempests move,
'Twere profanation of our joys
    To tell the laity our love.

Moving of th' Earth brings harms and fears,
    Men reckon what it did and meant;

But trepidation of the spheres,
  Though greater far, is innocent.

Dull sublunary lovers' love
  (Whose soul is sense) cannot admit
Absence, because it doth remove
  Those things which elemented it.

But we by a love so much refined
  That ourselves know not what it is,
Inter-assurèd of the mind,
  Care less, eyes, lips, and hands to miss.

Our two souls therefore, which are one,
  Though I must go, endure not yet
A breach, but an expansion,
  Like gold to aery thinness beat.

If they be two, they are two so
  As stiff twin compasses are two;
Thy soul the fixed foot makes no show
  To move, but doth, if th' other do.

And though it in the centre sit,
  Yet when the other far doth roam
It leans, and hearkens after it,
  And grows erect as that comes home.

Such wilt thou be to me, who must
  Like th' other foot obliquely run;
Thy firmness makes my circle just,
  And makes me end where I begun.

JOHN DONNE

Sonnet 7

At the round Earth's imagined corners, blow
Your trumpets, angels, and arise, arise
From death, you numberless infinities
Of souls, and to your scattered bodies go,
All whom the flood did, and fire shall o'erthrow,
All whom war, dearth, age, agues, tyrannies,
Despair, law, chance, hath slain, and you whose eyes
Shall behold God, and never taste death's woe.

But let them sleep, Lord, and me mourn a space,
For, if above all these my sins abound,
'Tis late to ask abundance of thy grace
When we are there; here on this lowly ground
Teach me how to repent; for that's as good
As if thou hadst sealed my pardon with thy blood.

JOHN DONNE

A Hymn to God the Father

Wilt thou forgive that sin where I begun,
   Which is my sin, though it were done before?
Wilt thou forgive that sin through which I run,
   And do run still, though still I do deplore?
      When thou hast done, thou hast not done,
       For I have more.

Wilt thou forgive that sin which I have won
   Others to sin? and made my sin their door?
Wilt thou forgive that sin which I did shun
   A year or two, but wallowed in, a score?
      When thou hast done, thou hast not done,
       For I have more.

I have a sin of fear, that when I have spun
   My last thread, I shall perish on the shore;
Swear by thyself, that at my death thy son
   Shall shine as he shines now and heretofore;
      And, having done that, thou hast done,
       I fear no more.

JOHN DONNE

Sonnet 14

Batter my heart, three-personed God; for you
As yet but knock, breathe, shine and seek to mend;
That I may rise, and stand, o'erthrow me, and bend
Your force, to break, blow, burn, and make me new.
I, like an usurped town to another due,
Labour to admit you, but oh, to no end:

Reason your viceroy in me, me should defend,
But is captived, and proves weak or untrue;
Yet dearly I love you, and would be loved fain,
But am betrothed unto your enemy:
Divorce me, untie, or break that knot again,
Take me to you, imprison me, for I
Except you enthral me, never shall be free,
Nor ever chaste, except you ravish me.

JOHN DONNE

The Apparition

When by thy scorn, O murderess, I am dead,
And that thou think'st thee free
From all solicitation from me,
Then shall my ghost come to thy bed,
And thee, feigned vestal, in worse arms shall see;
Then thy sick taper will begin to wink,
And he, whose thou art then, being tired before,
      Thou call'st for more,
And in false sleep will from thee shrink,
And then poor aspen wretch, neglected thou
Bathed in a cold quicksilver sweat wilt lie
      A verier ghost than I;
What I will say, I will not tell thee now,
Lest that preserve thee; and since my love is spent,
I had rather thou shouldst painfully repent,
Than by my threatenings rest still innocent.

JOHN DONNE

Good Friday, 1613. Riding Westward

Let man's soul be a sphere, and then, in this,
The intelligence that moves, devotion is;
And as the other spheres, by being grown
Subject to foreign motions, lose their own,
And being by others hurried every day,
Scarce in a year their natural form obey:

Pleasure or business, so, our souls admit
For their first mover, and are whirled by it.
Hence is't that I am carried towards the west
This day, when my soul's form bends to the east.
There I should see a sun by rising set,
And by that setting endless day beget;
But that Christ on this cross did rise and fall,
Sin had eternally benighted all.
Yet dare I almost be glad I do not see
That spectacle of too much weight for me.
Who sees God's face, that is self life, must die;
What a death were it then to see God die?
It made his own lieutenant nature shrink,
It made his footstool crack, and the sun wink.
Could I behold those hands which span the poles,
And turn all spheres at once, pierced with those holes?
Could I behold that endless height which is
Zenith to us, and our antipodes,
Humbled below us? or that blood which is
The seat of all our souls, if not of his,
Made dirt of dust, or that flesh which was worn
By God, for his apparel, ragged and torn?
If on these things I durst not look, durst I
Upon his miserable mother cast mine eye,
Who was God's partner here, and furnished thus
Half of that sacrifice which ransomed us?
Though these things, as I ride, be from mine eye,
They are present yet unto my memory,
For that looks towards them; and thou lookst towards me,
O Saviour, as thou hangst upon the tree;
I turn my back to thee but to receive
Corrections, till thy mercies bid thee leave.
Oh think me worth thine anger, punish me,
Burn off my rusts and my deformity,
Restore thine image so much, by thy grace,
That thou mayst know me, and I'll turn my face.

JOHN DONNE

Death be not proud, though some have callèd thee
Mighty and dreadful, for thou art not so;
For those whom thou thinkst thou dost overthrow
Die not, poor death, nor yet canst thou kill me;
From rest and sleep, which but thy pictures be,
Much pleasure, then from thee, much more must flow,
And soonest our best men with thee do go,
Rest of their bones, and soul's delivery.
Thou art slave to fate, chance, kings, and desperate men,
And dost with poison, war, and sickness dwell;
And poppy or charms can make us sleep as well
And better than thy stroke; why swellst thou then?
One short sleep past, we wake eternally,
And death shall be no more: death thou shalt die.

JOHN DONNE

[The Constant Lover]

Out upon it, I have loved
    Three whole days together,
And am like to love three more,
    If it hold fair weather.

Time shall moult away his wings
    Ere he shall discover
In the whole wide world again
    Such a constant lover.

But pox upon 't, no praise
    There is due at all to me:
Love with me had made no stay,
    Had it any been but she.

Had it any been but she
    And that very very face,
There had been at least ere this
    A dozen dozen in her place.

SIR JOHN SUCKLING

Song: To Lucasta,
Going to the Wars

Tell me not, sweet, I am unkind,
    That from the nunnery
Of thy chaste breast and quiet mind
    To war and arms I fly.

True: a new mistress now I chase,
    The first foe in the field;
And with a stronger faith embrace
    A sword, a horse, a shield.

Yet this inconstancy is such
    As you too shall adore;
I could not love thee, dear, so much,
    Loved I not honour more.

RICHARD LOVELACE

The Grasshopper

TO MY NOBLE FRIEND, MR CHARLES COTTON: ODE

O thou that swingst upon the waving hair
    Of some well-fillèd oaten beard,
Drunk every night with a delicious tear
    Dropped thee from heaven, where now th'art reared,

The joys of earth and air are thine entire,
    That with thy feet and wings dost hop and fly;
And when thy poppy works thou dost retire
    To thy carved acron bed to lie.

Up with the day, the sun thou welcom'st then,
    Sportst in the gilt plats of his beams,
And all these merry days mak'st merry men,
    Thyself, and melancholy streams.

But ah, the sickle! Golden ears are cropped;
    Ceres and Bacchus bid good night;
Sharp frosty fingers all your flowers have topped,
    And what scythes spared, winds shave off quite.

Poor verdant fool! And now green ice! Thy joys,
    Large and as lasting as thy perch of grass,
Bid us lay in 'gainst winter rain, and poise
    Their floods with an o'erflowing glass.

Thou best of men and friends! We will create
    A genuine summer in each other's breast;
And spite of this cold time and frozen fate
    Thaw us a warm seat to our rest.

Our sacred hearths shall burn eternally
    As Vestal flames: the north wind, he
Shall strike his frost-stretched wings, dissolve and fly
    This Etna in epitome.

Dropping December shall come weeping in,
    Bewail the usurping of his reign;
But when in showers of old Greek we begin,
    Shall cry he hath his crown again.

Night as clear Hesper shall our tapers whip
    From the light casements where we play,
And the dark hag from her black mantle strip,
    And stick there everlasting day.

Thus richer than untempted kings are we,
    That asking nothing, nothing need:
Though lord of all what seas embrace, yet he
    That wants himself is poor indeed.

RICHARD LOVELACE

La Bella Bona Roba

I cannot tell who loves the skeleton
Of a poor marmoset, nought but bone, bone.
Give me a nakedness with her clothes on:

Such whose white satin upper coat of skin,
Cut upon velvet rich incarnadine,
Has yet a body, and of flesh, within.

Sure it is meant good husbandry in men,
Who do incorporate with airy lean,
To repair their sides, and get their rib again.

Hard hap unto that huntsman that decrees
Fat joys for all his sweat, whenas he sees,
After his assay, nought but his keeper's fees.

Then, love, I beg, when next thou takest thy bow,
Thy angry shafts, and dost heart-chasing go,
Pass rascal deer, strike me the largest doe.

RICHARD LOVELACE

from *Lucasta*

TO LUCASTA

Like to the sentinel stars, I watch all night;
    For still the grand round of your light
        And glorious breast
        Awakes in me an east,
Nor will my rolling eyes e'er know a west.

Now on my down I'm tossed as on a wave,
    And my repose is made my grave;
        Fluttering I lie,
        Do beat myself and die,
But for a resurrection from your eye.

Ah my fair murderess! Dost thou cruelly heal,
    With various pains to make me well?
        Then let me be
        Thy cut anatomy,
And in each mangled part my heart you'll see.

RICHARD LOVELACE

My Picture Left in Scotland

I now think, Love is rather deaf, than blind,
    For else it could not be,
        That she,
Whom I adore so much, should so slight me,
    And cast my love behind:

I'm sure my language to her, was as sweet,
    And every close did meet
    In sentence, of as subtle feet,
        As hath the youngest he,
That sits in shadow of Apollo's tree.
Oh, but my conscious fears,
    That fly my thoughts between,
    Tell me that she hath seen
    My hundreds of grey hairs,
    Told seven and forty years,
Read so much waist, as she cannot embrace
My mountain belly, and my rocky face,
And all these through her eyes, have stopped her ears.

BEN JONSON

Song. To Celia

Come my Celia, let us prove,
While we may, the sports of love;
Time will not be ours, for ever:
He, at length, our good will sever.
Spend not then his gifts in vain.
Suns, that set, may rise again:
But if once we lose this light,
'Tis, with us, perpetual night.
Why should we defer our joys?
Fame, and rumour are but toys.
Cannot we delude the eyes
Of a few poor household spies?
Or his easier ears beguile,
So removèd by our wile?
'Tis no sin, love's fruit to steal,
But the sweet theft to reveal:
To be taken, to be seen,
These have crimes accounted been.

BEN JONSON

from *Cynthia's Revels*

Slow, slow, fresh fount, keep time with my salt tears;
    Yet slower yet, oh faintly, gentle springs;
List to the heavy part the music bears:
    Woe weeps out her division when she sings.
        Droop, herbs and flowers,
        Fall, grief, in showers;
        Our beauties are not ours:
            Oh, I could still,
Like melting snow upon some craggy hill,
    Drop, drop, drop, drop,
Since nature's pride is now a withered daffodil.

BEN JONSON

from *Epicoene*

    Still to be neat, still to be dressed,
    As you were going to a feast;
    Still to be powdered, still perfúmed:
    Lady, it is to be presumed,
    Though art's hid causes are not found,
    All is not sweet, all is not sound.

    Give me a look, give me a face,
    That makes simplicity a grace;
    Robes loosely flowing, hair as free:
    Such sweet neglect more taketh me
    Than all the adulteries of art:
    They strike mine eyes, but not my heart.

BEN JONSON

from *The New Inn*

[VISION OF BEAUTY]

It was a beauty that I saw
So pure, so perfect, as the frame
Of all the universe was lame;
To that one figure, could I draw,
Or give least line of it a law!

A skein of silk without a knot!
A fair march made without a halt!
A curious form without a fault!
A printed book without a blot!
All beauty, and without a spot!

BEN JONSON

from *The Forest*

II: TO PENSHURST

Thou art not, Penshurst, built to envious show,
Of touch or marble, nor canst boast a row
Of polished pillars, or a roof of gold;
Thou hast no lantern whereof tales are told,
Or stair, or courts; but standst an ancient pile,
And these grudged at, art reverenced the while.
Thou joy'st in better marks, of soil, of air,
Of wood, of water; therein thou art fair.
Thou hast thy walks for health as well as sport:
Thy Mount, to which the dryads do resort,
Where Pan and Bacchus their high feasts have made
Beneath the broad beech and the chestnut shade;
That taller tree, which of a nut was set
At his great birth, where all the Muses met.
There, in the writhèd bark, are cut the names
Of many a sylvan, taken with his flames;
And thence the ruddy satyrs oft provoke
The lighter fauns to reach thy lady's oak.
Thy copse, too, named of Gamage, thou hast there,
That never fails to serve thee seasoned deer
When thou wouldst feast or exercise thy friends.

The lower land, that to the river bends,
Thy sheep, thy bullocks, kine and calves do feed;
The middle grounds thy mares and horses breed.
Each bank doth yield thee conies, and the tops,
Fertile of wood, Ashour and Sidney's copse,
To crown thy open table, doth provide
The purpled pheasant with the speckled side;
The painted partridge lies in every field,
And for thy mess is willing to be killed.
And if the high-swoll'n Medway fail thy dish,
Thou hast thy ponds that pay thee tribute fish:
Fat, agéd carps, that run into thy net;
And pikes, now weary their own kind to eat,
As loth the second draught or cast to stay,
Officiously, at first, themselves betray;
Bright eels, that emulate them, and leap on land
Before the fisher, or into his hand.
Then hath thy orchard fruit, thy garden flowers,
Fresh as the air and new as are the Hours:
The early cherry, with the later plum,
Fig, grape and quince, each in his time doth come;
The blushing apricot and woolly peach
Hang on thy walls, that every child may reach.
And though thy walls be of the country stone,
They're reared of no man's ruin, no man's groan;
There's none that dwell about them wish them down,
But all come in, the farmer and the clown,
And no one empty-handed, to salute
Thy lord and lady, though they have no suit.
Some bring a capon, some a rural cake,
Some nuts, some apples; some that think they make
The better cheeses, bring them; or else send
By their ripe daughters, whom they would commend
This way to husbands; and whose baskets bear
An emblem of themselves, in plum or pear.
But what can this (more than express their love)
Add to thy free provisions, far above
The need of such? whose liberal board doth flow,
With all that hospitality doth know!
Where comes no guest but is allowed to eat
Without his fear, and of thy lord's own meat;

24

Where the same beer and bread and self-same wine
That is his lordship's shall be also mine;
And I not fain to sit (as some, this day,
At great men's tables) and yet dine away.
Here no man tells my cups, nor, standing by,
A waiter, doth my gluttony envy,
But gives me what I call, and lets me eat;
He knows below he shall find plenty of meat,
Thy tables hoard not up for the next day.
Nor, when I take my lodging, need I pray
For fire or lights or livery: all is there,
As if thou then wert mine, or I reigned here;
There's nothing I can wish, for which I stay.
That found King James, when, hunting late this way
With his brave son, the prince, they saw thy fires
Shine bright on every hearth, as the desires
Of thy Penates had been set on flame
To entertain them; or the country came
With all their zeal to warm their welcome here.
What (great, I will not say, but) sudden cheer
Didst thou then make them! And what praise was heaped
On thy good lady then! who therein reaped
The just reward of her high huswifery:
To have her linen, plate, and all things nigh,
When she was far; and not a room but dressed
As if it had expected such a guest!
These, Penshurst, are thy praise, and yet not all.
Thy lady's noble, fruitful, chaste withal;
His children thy great lord may call his own,
A fortune in this age but rarely known.
They are and have been taught religion; thence
Their gentler spirits have sucked innocence.
Each morn and even they are taught to pray
With the whole household, and may every day
Read in their virtuous parents' noble parts
The mysteries of manners, arms and arts.
Now, Penshurst, they that will proportion thee
With other edifices, when they see
Those proud, ambitious heaps, and nothing else,
May say, their lords have built, but thy lord dwells.

BEN JONSON

from *The White Devil*

Call for the robin redbreast and the wren,
Since o'er shady groves they hover,
And with leaves and flowers do cover
The friendless bodies of unburied men.
Call unto his funeral dole
The ant, the field-mouse and the mole,
To rear him hillocks, that shall keep him warm
And (when gay tombs are robbed) sustain no harm.
But keep the wolf far thence, that's foe to men,
For with his nails he'll dig them up again.

JOHN WEBSTER

An Ode. To Himself

Where dost thou careless lie,
   Buried in ease and sloth?
Knowledge that sleeps doth die;
And this security,
     It is the common moth,
That eats on wits, and arts, and oft destroys them both.

Are all the Aonian springs
   Dried up? Lies Thespia waste?
Doth Clarius' harp want strings,
That not a nymph now sings?
     Or droop they, as disgraced
To see their seats and bowers by chattering pies defaced?

If hence thy silence be,
   As 'tis too just a cause,
Let this thought quicken thee:
Minds that are great and free
     Should not on fortune pause;
'Tis crown enough to virtue still, her own applause.

What though the greedy fry
   Be taken with false baits
Of worded balladry,

And think it poesy?
    They die with their conceits,
And only piteous scorn upon their folly waits.

Then take in hand thy lyre,
    Strike in thy proper strain;
With Japhet's line, aspire
Sol's chariot for new fire
    To give the world again;
Who aided him, will thee, the issue of Jove's brain.

And since our dainty age
    Cannot endure reproof,
Make not thyself a page
To that strumpet, the stage;
    But sing high and aloof,
Safe from the wolf's black jaw, and the dull ass's hoof.

BEN JONSON

L'Allegro

Hence, loathèd melancholy,
    Of Cerberus and blackest midnight born,
In Stygian cave forlorn
    'Mongst horrid shapes, and shrieks, and sights unholy;
Find out some uncouth cell,
    Where brooding darkness spreads his jealous wings,
And the night-raven sings:
    There under ebon shades, and low-browed rocks
As ragged as thy locks,
    In dark Cimmerian desert ever dwell.
But come, thou goddess fair and free,
In heaven yclept Euphrosynë,
And by men, heart-easing mirth,
Whom lovely Venus at a birth
With two sister Graces more
To ivy-crownèd Bacchus bore;
Or whether (as some sager sing)
The frolic wind that breathes the spring,
Zephyr with Aurora playing,
As he met her once a-Maying,

There on beds of violets blue
And fresh-blown roses washed in dew,
Filled her with thee, a daughter fair,
So buxom, blithe, and debonair.
Haste thee nymph, and bring with thee
Jest and youthful jollity,
Quips and cranks, and wanton wiles,
Nods, and becks, and wreathèd smiles
Such as hang on Hebe's cheek
And love to live in dimple sleek;
Sport that wrinkled care derides,
And laughter holding both his sides.
Come, and trip it as you go
On the light fantastic toe,
And in thy right hand lead with thee
The mountain nymph, sweet liberty;
And if I give thee honour due,
Mirth, admit me of thy crew
To live with her, and live with thee,
In unreprovèd pleasures free;
To hear the lark begin his flight,
And singing startle the dull night
From his watch-tower in the skies,
Till the dappled dawn doth rise;
Then to come in spite of sorrow,
And at my window bid good morrow,
Through the sweet-briar, or the vine,
Or the twisted eglantine;
While the cock with lively din
Scatters the rear of darkness thin,
And to the stack, or the barn door,
Stoutly struts his dames before,
Oft listening how the hounds and horn
Cheerly rouse the slumbering morn
From the side of some hoar hill,
Through the high wood echoing shrill.
Sometime walking not unseen
By hedgerow elms on hillocks green,
Right against the eastern gate
Where the great sun begins his state,
Robed in flames and amber light,

The clouds in thousand liveries dight;
While the ploughman near at hand
Whistles o'er the furrowed land,
And the milkmaid singeth blithe,
And the mower whets his scythe,
And every shepherd tells his tale
Under the hawthorn in the dale.
Straight mine eye hath caught new pleasures
Whilst the landscape round it measures:
Russet lawns and fallows grey
Where the nibbling flocks do stray,
Mountains on whose barren breast
The labouring clouds do often rest;
Meadows trim with daisies pied,
Shallow brooks and rivers wide.
Towers and battlements it sees
Bosomed high in tufted trees,
Where perhaps some beauty lies,
The cynosure of neighbouring eyes.
Hard by, a cottage chimney smokes
From betwixt two agèd oaks,
Where Corydon and Thyrsis met
Are at their savoury dinner set
Of herbs and other country messes,
Which the neat-handed Phillis dresses;
And then in haste her bower she leaves,
With Thestylis to bind the sheaves;
Or if the earlier season lead
To the tanned haycock in the mead,
Sometimes with secure delight
The upland hamlets will invite,
When the merry bells ring round,
And the jocund rebecks sound
To many a youth and many a maid,
Dancing in the chequered shade;
And young and old come forth to play
On a sunshine holiday,
Till the livelong daylight fail.
Then to the spicy nut-brown ale,
With stories told of many a feat:
How Faëry Mab the junkets eat,

She was pinched and pulled she said,
And by the friar's lantern led
Tells how the drudging goblin sweat
To earn his cream-bowl duly set,
When in one night, ere glimpse of morn,
His shadowy flail hath threshed the corn
That ten day-labourers could not end;
Then lies him down the lubber fiend,
And, stretched out all the chimney's length,
Basks at the fire his hairy strength;
And crop-full out of doors he flings,
Ere the first cock his matin rings.
Thus done the tales, to bed they creep,
By whispering winds soon lulled asleep.
Towered cities please us then,
And the busy hum of men,
Where throngs of knights and barons bold,
In weeds of peace high triumphs hold,
With store of ladies, whose bright eyes
Rain influence, and judge the prize
Of wit, or arms, while both contend
To win her grace, whom all commend.
There let Hymen oft appear
In saffron robe, with taper clear,
And pomp, and feast, and revelry,
With mask, and antique pageantry:
Such sights as youthful poets dream
On summer eves by haunted stream.
Then to the well-trod stage anon,
If Jonson's learned sock be on,
Or sweetest Shakespeare fancy's child
Warble his native wood-notes wild,
And ever against eating cares
Lap me in soft Lydian airs,
Married to immortal verse
Such as the meeting soul may pierce
In notes, with many a winding bout
Of linkèd sweetness long drawn out,
With wanton heed, and giddy cunning,
The melting voice through mazes running;
Untwisting all the chains that tie

The hidden soul of harmony,
That Orpheus' self may heave his head
From golden slumber on a bed
Of heaped Elysian flowers, and hear
Such strains as would have won the ear
Of Pluto, to have quite set free
His half-regained Eurydicë.
These delights, if thou canst give,
Mirth with thee I mean to live.

JOHN MILTON

To the Virgins, to Make Much of Time

Gather ye rosebuds while ye may,
   Old Time is still a-flying;
And this same flower that smiles today,
   Tomorrow will be dying.

The glorious lamp of heaven, the sun,
   The higher he's a getting;
The sooner will his race be run,
   And nearer he's to setting.

That age is best which is the first,
   When youth and blood are warmer;
But being spent, the worse, and worst
   Times, still succeed the former.

Then be not coy, but use your time,
   And while ye may, go marry;
For having lost but once your prime,
   You may for ever tarry.

ROBERT HERRICK

Corinna's going a-Maying

Get up, get up for shame, the blooming morn
Upon her wings presents the god unshorn
   See how Aurora throws her fair
   Fresh-quilted colours through the air:
   Get up, sweet slug-a-bed, and see

31

The dew bespangling herb and tree.
Each flower has wept, and bowed toward the East
Above an hour since; yet you not dressed,
    Nay! not so much as out of bed?
    When all the birds have matins said,
    And sung their thankful hymns: 'tis sin,
    Nay, profanation to keep in,
When as a thousand virgins on this day,
Spring, sooner than the lark, to fetch in May.

Rise, and put on your foliage, and be seen
To come forth, like the spring-time, fresh and green;
    And sweet as Flora. Take no care
    For jewels for your gown, or hair:
    Fear not, the leaves will strew
    Gems in abundance upon you:
Besides, the childhood of the day has kept,
Against you come, some orient pearls unwept:
    Come and receive them while the light
    Hangs on the dew-locks of the night,
    And Titan on the eastern hill
    Retires himself, or else stands still
Till you come forth. Wash, dress, be brief in praying:
Few beads are best, when once we go a-Maying.

Come, my Corinna, come; and coming, mark
How each field turns a street; each street a park
    Made green, and trimmed with trees: see how
    Devotion gives each house a bough,
    Or branch. Each porch, each door, ere this,
    An ark, a tabernacle is
Made up of white-thorn, neatly interwove,
As if here were those cooler shades of love.
    Can such delights be in the street,
    And open fields, and we not see't?
    Come, we'll abroad, and let's obey
    The proclamation made for May:
And sin no more, as we have done, by staying;
But my Corinna, come, let's go a-Maying.

There's not a budding boy, or girl, this day,
But is got up, and gone to bring in May.

A deal of youth, ere this, is come
Back, and with white-thorn laden home.
 Some have despatched their cakes and cream,
 Before that we have left to dream:
And some have wept, and wooed, and plighted troth,
And chose their priest, ere we can cast off sloth.
 Many a green-gown has been given;
 Many a kiss, both odd and even:
 Many a glance too has been sent
 From out the eye, love's firmament:
Many a jest told of the keys betraying
This night, and locks picked, yet we're not a-Maying.

Come, let us go, while we are in our prime;
And take the harmless folly of the time.
 We shall grow old apace, and die
 Before we know our liberty.
 Our life is short; and our days run
 As fast away as does the sun:
And as a vapour, or a drop of rain
Once lost, can ne'er be found again:
 So when or you or I are made
 A fable, song, or fleeting shade;
 All love, all liking, all delight
 Lies drowned with us in endless night.
Then while time serves, and we are but decaying;
Come, my Corinna, come, let's go a Maying.

ROBERT HERRICK

Delight in Disorder

 A sweet disorder in the dress
 Kindles in clothes a wantonness:
 A lawn about the shoulders thrown
 Into a fine distraction;
 An erring lace, which here and there
 Enthrals the crimson stomacher;
 A cuff neglectful, and thereby
 Ribbands to flow confusèdly;
 A winning wave (deserving note)

In the tempestuous petticoat;
A careless shoestring, in whose tie
I see a wild civility:
Do more bewitch me, than when art
Is too precise in every part.

ROBERT HERRICK

To Blossoms

Fair pledges of a fruitful tree,
    Why do ye fall so fast?
    Your date is not so past;
But you may stay yet here a while,
    To blush and gently smile;
        And go at last.

What, were ye born to be
    An hour or half's delight;
    And so to bid goodnight?
'Twas pity Nature brought ye forth
    Merely to show your worth,
        And lose you quite.

But you are lovely Leaves, where we
    May read how soon things have
    Their end, though ne'er so brave:
And after they have shown their pride,
    Like you a while: they glide
        Into the grave.

ROBERT HERRICK

Madrigal 1.3

Like the Idalian queen,
Her hair about her eyne,
With neck and breasts ripe apples to be seen,
At first glance of the morn
In Cyprus gardens gathering those fair flowers
Which of her blood were born,
I saw, but fainting saw, my paramours.

The Graces naked danced about the place,
The winds and trees amazed
With silence on her gazed;
The flowers did smile, like those upon her face,
And as their aspen stalks those fingers band,
That she might read my case,
A hyacinth I wished me in her hand.

WILLIAM DRUMMOND OF HAWTHORNDEN

[Hymn to Cynthia]

Queen and huntress, chaste and fair,
Now the sun is laid to sleep,
Seated in thy silver chair,
State in wonted manner keep:
    Hesperus entreats thy light,
    Goddess excellently bright.

Earth, let not thy envious shade
Dare itself to interpose;
Cynthia's shining orb was made
Heaven to clear, when day did close:
    Bless us then with wishèd sight,
    Goddess excellently bright.

Lay thy bow of pearl apart,
And thy crystal-shining quiver;
Give unto the flying hart
Space to breathe, how short soever:
    Thou that mak'st a day of night,
    Goddess excellently bright.

BEN JONSON

Sonnet 2.12

As, in a dusky and tempestuous night,
A star is wont to spread her locks of gold,
And while her pleasant rays abroad are rolled,
Some spiteful cloud doth rob us of her sight;
Fair soul, in this black age so shined thou bright,

And made all eyes with wonder thee behold,
Till ugly death, depriving us of light,
In his grim misty arms thee did enfold.
Who more shall vaunt true beauty here to see?
What hope doth more in any heart remain,
That such perfections shall his reason rein,
If beauty, with thee born, too died with thee?
    World, plain no more of love, nor count his harms;
    With his pale trophies death hath hung his arms.

WILLIAM DRUMMOND OF HAWTHORNDEN

Il Penseroso

Hence, vain deluding joys,
    The brood of folly without father bred;
How little you bestead,
    Or fill the fixèd mind with all your toys:
Dwell in some idle brain,
    And fancies fond with gaudy shapes possess,
As thick and numberless
    As the gay motes that people the sunbeams,
Or likest hovering dreams
    The fickle pensioners of Morpheus' train.
But hail thou goddess, sage and holy,
Hail divinest melancholy,
Whose saintly visage is too bright
To hit the sense of human sight,
And therefore to our weaker view
O'erlaid with black, staid wisdom's hue:
Black, but such as in esteem
Prince Memnon's sister might beseem,
Or that starred Ethiop queen that strove
To set her beauty's praise above
The sea-nymphs, and their powers offended.
Yet thou art higher far descended:
Thee bright-haired Vesta long of yore,
To solitary Saturn bore;
His daughter she (in Saturn's reign,
Such mixture was not held a stain).
Oft in glimmering bowers and glades

36

He met her, and in secret shades
Of woody Ida's inmost grove,
Whilst yet there was no fear of Jove.
Come pensive nun, devout and pure,
Sober, steadfast, and demure,
All in a robe of darkest grain,
Flowing with majestic train,
And sable stole of cypress lawn
Over thy decent shoulders drawn.
Come, but keep thy wonted state,
With even step, and musing gait,
And looks commercing with the skies,
Thy rapt soul sitting in thine eyes:
There held in holy passion still
Forget thyself to marble, till
With a sad leaden downward cast
Thou fix them on the earth as fast.
And join with thee calm peace, and quiet,
Spare fast, that oft with gods doth diet,
And hears the Muses in a ring
Ay round about Jove's altar sing.
And add to these retirèd leisure,
That in trim gardens takes his pleasure;
But first, and chiefest, with thee bring
Him that yon soars on golden wing,
Guiding the fiery-wheelèd throne,
The cherub contemplation;
And the mute silence hist along,
'Less Philomel will deign a song,
In her sweetest, saddest plight,
Smoothing the rugged brow of night,
While Cynthia checks her dragon yoke,
Gently o'er the accustomed oak:
Sweet bird that shunn'st the noise of folly,
Most musical, most melancholy!
Thee chauntress oft the woods among
I woo to hear thy evensong;
And missing thee, I walk unseen
On the dry smooth-shaven green,
To behold the wandering moon
Riding near her highest noon,

Like one that had been led astray
Through the heaven's wide pathless way;
And oft, as if her head she bowed,
Stooping through a fleecy cloud.
Oft on a plat of rising ground,
I hear the far-off curfew sound
Over some wide-waterèd shore,
Swinging slow with sullen roar;
Or if the air will not permit,
Some still removèd place will fit,
Where glowing embers through the room
Teach light to counterfeit a gloom,
Far from all resort of mirth,
Save the cricket on the hearth,
Or the bellman's drowsy charm,
To bless the doors from nightly harm;
Or let my lamp at midnight hour
Be seen in some high lonely tower,
Where I may oft outwatch the Bear,
With thrice great Hermes, or unsphere
The spirit of Plato to unfold
What worlds or what vast regions hold
The immortal mind that hath forsook
Her mansion in this fleshly nook;
And of those demons that are found
In fire, air, flood, or under ground,
Whose power hath a true consent
With planet or with element.
Sometime let gorgeous tragedy
In sceptred pall come sweeping by,
Presenting Thebes, or Pelops' line,
Or the tale of Troy divine.
Or what (though rare) of later age
Ennobled hath the buskined stage.
But, O sad virgin, that thy power
Might raise Musaeus from his bower,
Or bid the soul of Orpheus sing
Such notes as warbled to the string
Drew iron tears down Pluto's cheek,
And made hell grant what love did seek.
Or call up him that left half-told

The story of Cambuscan bold,
Of Camball, and of Algarsife,
And who had Canace to wife,
That owned the virtuous ring and glass,
And of the wondrous horse of brass,
On which the Tartar king did ride;
And if aught else great bards beside
In sage and solemn tunes have sung,
Of tourneys and of trophies hung;
Of forests and enchantments drear,
Where more is meant than meets the ear,
Thus night oft see me in thy pale career,
Till civil-suited morn appear,
Not tricked and frounced as she was wont,
With the Attic boy to hunt,
But kerchiefed in a comely cloud,
While rocking winds are piping loud,
Or ushered with a shower still,
When the gust hath blown his fill,
Ending on the rustling leaves,
With minute drops from off the eaves.
And when the sun begins to fling
His flaring beams, me goddess bring
To archèd walks of twilight groves,
And shadows brown that Sylvan loves
Of pine, or monumental oak,
Where the rude axe with heavèd stroke,
Was never heard the nymphs to daunt,
Or fright them from their hallowed haunt.
There in close covert by some brook,
Where no profaner eye may look,
Hide me from day's garish eye,
While the bee with honied thigh,
That at her flowery work doth sing,
And the waters murmuring
With such consort as they keep,
Entice the dewy-feathered sleep;
And let some strange mysterious dream,
Wave at his wings in airy stream,
Of lively portraiture displayed,
Softly on my eyelids laid.

And as I wake, sweet music breathe
Above, about, or underneath,
Sent by some spirit to mortals good,
Or the unseen genius of the wood.
But let my due feet never fail
To walk the studious cloisters pale,
And love the high embowèd roof,
With antique pillars' massy proof,
And storied windows richly dight,
Casting a dim religious light.
There let the pealing organ blow
To the full-voiced choir below
In service high and anthems clear,
As may with sweetness, through mine ear,
Dissolve me into ecstasies,
And bring all heaven before mine eyes.
And may at last my weary age
Find out the peaceful hermitage,
The hairy gown and mossy cell,
Where I may sit and rightly spell
Of every star that heaven doth shew,
And every herb that sips the dew;
Till old experience do attain
To something like prophetic strain.
These pleasures melancholy give,
And I with thee will choose to live.

JOHN MILTON

To Meadows

Ye have been fresh and green,
    Ye have been filled with flowers;
And ye the walks have been
    Where maids have spent their hours.

You have beheld how they
    With wicker arks did come
To kiss, and bear away
    The richer cowslips home.

You've heard them sweetly sing,
    And seen them in a round:
Each virgin, like a spring,
    With honeysuckles crowned.

But now, we see, none here,
    Whose silvery feet did tread,
And with dishevelled hair
    Adorned this smoother mead.

Like unthrifts, having spent
    Your stock, and needy grown,
You're left here to lament
    Your poor estates, alone.

ROBERT HERRICK

The Argument of His Book

I sing of brooks, of blossoms, birds and bowers:
Of April, May, of June, and July-flowers.
I sing of maypoles, hock-carts, wassails, wakes,
Of bride-grooms, brides, and of their bridal-cakes.
I write of youth, of love, and have access
By these, to sing of cleanly-wantonness.
I sing of dews, of rains, and piece by piece
Of balm, of oil, of spice and ambergris.
I sing of times trans-shifting; and I write
How roses first came red, and lilies white.
I write of groves, of twilights, and I sing
The court of Mab, and of the fairy-king.
I write of Hell; I sing (and ever shall)
Of Heaven, and hope to have it after all.

ROBERT HERRICK

To Daffodils

Fair daffodils, we weep to see
    You haste away so soon:
As yet the early-rising sun
    Has not attained his noon.

Stay, stay,
Until the hasting day
Has run
But to the evensong,
And, having prayed together, we
Will go with you along.

We have short time to stay as you,
We have as short a spring;
As quick a growth to meet decay
As you, or any thing.
We die,
As your hours do, and dry
Away,
Like to the summer's rain,
Or as the pearls of morning's dew
Ne'er to be found again.

ROBERT HERRICK

Upon Julia's Clothes

Whenas in silks my Julia goes,
Then, then (methinks) how sweetly flows
That liquefaction of her clothes.

Next, when I cast mine eyes and see
That brave vibration each way free,
Oh how that glittering taketh me!

ROBERT HERRICK

Her Legs

Fain would I kiss my Julia's dainty leg,
Which is as white and hairless as an egg.

ROBERT HERRICK

Cherry-ripe

Cherry-ripe, ripe, ripe, I cry,
Full and fair ones; come and buy:
If so be, you ask me where
They do grow? I answer, there,
Where my Julia's lips do smile;
There's the land, or cherry-isle:
Whose plantations fully show
All the year, where cherries grow.

ROBERT HERRICK

Upon His Departure Hence

Thus I
Pass by,
And die:
As one,
Unknown,
And gone:
I'm made
A shade,
And laid
I'th' grave,
There have
My cave.
Where tell
I dwell
Farewell.

ROBERT HERRICK

The Nightpiece, to Julia

Her eyes the glow-worm lend thee,
The shooting stars attend thee;
 And the elves also,
 Whose little eyes glow
Like the sparks of fire, befriend thee.

No will-o'the-wisp mislight thee,
Nor snake or slow-worm bite thee;
   But on, on thy way
   Not making a stay,
Since ghost there's none to affright thee.

Let not the dark thee cumber;
What though the moon does slumber?
   The stars of the night
   Will lend thee their light,
Like tapers clear without number.

Then Julia let me woo thee,
Thus, thus to come unto me;
   And when I shall meet
   Thy silvery feet,
My soul I'll pour into thee.

ROBERT HERRICK

To Julia

Julia, when thy Herrick dies,
Close thou up thy poet's eyes;
And his last breath, let it be
Taken in by none but thee.

ROBERT HERRICK

How Roses Came Red

Roses at first were white,
   Till they could not agree,
Whether my Sappho's breast,
   Or they more white should be.

But being vanquished quite,
   A blush their cheeks bespread;
Since which (believe the rest)
   The roses first came red.

ROBERT HERRICK

'Doing a filthy pleasure is'

Doing, a filthy pleasure is, and short;
And done, we straight repent us of the sport:
Let us not then rush blindly on unto it,
Like lustful beasts, that only know to do it:
For lust will languish, and that heat decay,
But thus, thus, keeping endless holiday,
Let us together closely lie, and kiss,
There is no labour, nor no shame in this;
This hath pleased, doth please, and long will please; never
Can this decay, but is beginning ever.

BEN JONSON

'My Beloved is Mine, and I am His; He Feedeth Among the Lilies'

E'en like two little bank-dividing brooks,
    That wash the pebbles with their wanton streams,
And having rang'd and search'd a thousand nooks,
    Meet both at length in silver-breasted Thames,
        Where in a greater current they conjoin:
So I my best belovèd's am; so he is mine.

E'en so we met; and after long pursuit,
    E'en so we joined, we both became entire;
No need for either to renew the suit,
    For I was flax, and he was flames of fire.
        Our firm united souls did more than twine:
So I my best belovèd's am; so he is mine.

If all those glitt'ring monarchs that command
    The servile quarters of this earthly ball
Should tender, in exchange, their shares of land,
    I would not change my fortunes for them all:
        Their wealth is but a counter to my coin:
The world's but theirs; but my belovèd's mine.

Nay more; if the fair Thespian ladies all
    Should heap together their diviner treasure,

45

That treasure should be deemed a price too small
　To buy a minute's lease of half my pleasure;
　　'Tis not the sacred wealth of all the Nine
Can buy my heart from him, or his from being mine.

Nor time, nor place, nor chance, nor death can bow
　My least desires unto the least remove;
He's firmly mine by oath, I his by vow,
　He's mine by faith, and I am his by love;
　　He's mine by water, I am his by wine:
Thus I my best belovèd's am; thus he is mine.

He is my altar, I his holy place;
　I am his guest, and he my living food;
I'm his by penitence, he mine by grace;
　I'm his by purchase, he is mine by blood;
　　He's my supporting helm, and I his vine:
Thus I my best belovèd's am; thus he is mine.

He gives me wealth, I give him all my vows;
　I give him songs, he gives me length of days;
With wreaths of grace he crowns my conquering brows,
　And I his temples with a crown of praise,
　　Which he accepts—an everlasting sign,
That I my best belovèd's am; that he is mine.

FRANCIS QUARLES

Redemption

Having been tenant long to a rich lord,
　Not thriving, I resolvèd to be bold,
　And make a suit unto him, to afford
A new small-rented lease, and cancel the old.
In heaven at his manor I him sought:
　They told me there that he was lately gone
　About some land, which he had dearly bought
Long since on earth, to take possession.
I straight returned, and knowing his great birth
　Sought him accordingly in great resorts:
　In cities, theatres, gardens, parks, and courts.
At length I heard a ragged noise and mirth

Of thieves and murderers: there I him espied,
Who straight, 'Your suit is granted', said, and died.

GEORGE HERBERT

The Agony

Philosophers have measured mountains,
Fathomed the depths of seas, of states, and kings,
Walked with a staff to heav'n, and traced fountains:
    But there are two vast, spacious things,
The which to measure it doth more behove:
Yet few there are that sound them; Sin and Love.

    Who would know Sin, let him repair
Unto Mount Olivet; there shall he see
A man so wrung with pains, that all his hair,
    His skin, his garments bloody be.
Sin is that press and vice, which forceth pain
To hunt his cruel food through ev'ry vein.

    Who knows not Love, let him assay
And taste that juice, which on the cross a pike
Did set again abroach; then let him say
    If ever he did taste the like.
Love is that liquor sweet and most divine,
Which my god feels as blood; but I, as wine.

GEORGE HERBERT

Life

I made a posy, while the day ran by:
Here will I smell my remnant out, and tie
    My life within this band.
But time did beckon to the flowers, and they
By noon most cunningly did steal away,
    And withered in my hand.

My hand was next to them, and then my heart:
I took, without more thinking, in good part
    Time's gentle admonition:
Who did so sweetly death's sad taste convey,

Making my mind to smell my fatal day;
        Yet sug'ring the suspicìon.

Farewell dear flowers: sweetly your time ye spent,
Fit, while ye lived, for smell or ornament,
        And after death for cures.
I follow straight without complaints or grief,
Since if my scent be good, I care not if
        It be as short as yours.

GEORGE HERBERT

Prayer (I)

Prayer, the Church's banquet, angel's age,
  God's breath in man returning to his birth,
  The soul in paraphrase, heart in pilgrimage,
The Christian plummet sounding heaven and Earth:
Engine against th' almighty, sinner's tower,
  Reversèd thunder, Christ-side-piercing spear,
  The six-days world transposing in an hour,
A kind of tune, which all things hear and fear;
Softness, and peace, and joy, and love, and bliss,
  Exalted manna, gladness of the best,
  Heaven in ordinary, man well dressed,
The Milky Way, the bird of paradise,
  Church-bells beyond the stars heard, the soul's blood,
  The land of spices; something understood.

GEORGE HERBERT

Virtue

Sweet day, so cool, so calm, so bright,
The bridal of the earth and sky:
The dew shall weep thy fall tonight;
        For thou must die.

Sweet rose, whose hue angry and brave
Bids the rash gazer wipe his eye:
Thy root is ever in its grave,
        And thou must die.

Sweet spring, full of sweet days and roses,
A box where sweets compacted lie:
My music shows ye have your closes,
        And all must die.

Only a sweet and virtuous soul,
Like seasoned timber, never gives;
But though the whole world turn to coal,
        Then chiefly lives.

GEORGE HERBERT

[Sonnett 11: For the Baptist]

The last and greatest herald of heaven's king,
Girt with rough skins, hies to the deserts wild,
Among that savage brook the woods forth bring,
Which he than man more harmless found and mild:
His food was locusts, and what young doth spring,
With honey that from virgin hives distilled;
Parched body, hollow eyes, some uncouth thing
Made him appear, long since from Earth exiled.
There burst he forth: 'All ye whose hopes rely
On God, with me amidst these deserts mourn;
Repent, repent, and from old errors turn.'
Who listened to his voice, obeyed his cry?
    Only the echoes, which he made relent,
    Rung from their marble caves, 'Repent, repent!'

WILLIAM DRUMMOND OF HAWTHORNDEN

The Pilgrimage

I travelled on, seeing the hill, where lay
        My expectation.
    A long it was and weary way.
    The gloomy cave of desperation
I left on th' one, and on the other side
        The rock of pride.

And so I came to fancy's meadow strowed
        With many a flower:

49

Fain would I here have made abode,
     But I was quickened by my hour.
So to care's copse I came, and there got through
          With much ado.

That led me to the wild of passion, which
          Some call the wold:
     A wasted place, but sometimes rich.
     Here I was robbed of all my gold,
Save one good angel, which a friend had tied
          Close to my side.

At length I got unto the gladsome hill,
          Where lay my hope,
     Where lay my heart; and climbing still,
     When I had gained the brow and top,
A lake of brackish waters on the ground
          Was all I found.

With that abashed and struck with many a sting
          Of swarming fears,
     I fell, and cried, Alas my King!
          Can both the way and end be tears?
Yet taking heart I rose, and then perceived
          I was deceived:

My hill was further: so I flung away,
          Yet heard a cry,
     Just as I went, 'None goes that way
     And lives': If that be all, said I,
After so foul a journey death is fair,
          And but a chair.

GEORGE HERBERT

On the Death of Mr Purcell

Mark how the lark and linnet sing,
     With rival notes
They strain their warbling throats
     To welcome in the spring.
     But in the close of night,
When Philomel begins her heavenly lay,

They cease their mutual spite,
Drink in her music with delight,
And list'ning and silent, and silent and list'ning,
    And list'ning and silent obey.

    So ceased the rival crew, when Purcell came,
    They sung no more, or only sung his fame.
      Struck dumb, they all admired
        The godlike man,
      Alas, too soon retired,
        As he too late began.
We beg not hell our Orpheus to restore;
    Had he been there,
    Their sovereigns' fear
Had sent him back before.
The power of harmony too well they knew;
He long e'er this had tuned their jarring sphere,
        And left no hell below.

The heavenly quire, who heard his notes from high,
Let down the scale of music from the sky:
    They handed him along,
And all the way he taught, and all the way they sung.
Ye brethren of the lyre and tuneful voice,
Lament his lot: but at your own rejoice.
Now live secure, and linger out your days,
The gods are pleased alone with Purcell's lays,
    Nor know to mend their choice.

                JOHN DRYDEN

An Exequy to His Matchless Never-to-be-forgotten Friend

Accept, thou shrine of my dead saint,
Instead of dirges this complaint!
And for sweet flowers to crown thy hearse
Receive a strew of weeping verse
From thy grieved friend, whom thou mightst see
Quite melted into tears for thee.
    Dear loss! Since thy untimely fate
My task hath been to meditate

On thee, on thee: thou art the book,
The library whereon I look,
Though almost blind. For thee (loved clay!)
I languish out, not live the day,
Using no other exercise
But what I practise with mine eyes.
By which wet glasses I find out
How lazily time creeps about
The one that mourns. This, only this
My exercise and business is:
So I compute the weary hours
With sighs dissolvèd into showers.

   Nor wonder if my time go thus
Backward and most preposterous;
Thou has benighted me. Thy set
This eve of blackness did beget,
Who wast my day (though overcast
Before thou hadst thy noontide passed),
And I remember must in tears,
Thou scarce hadst seen so many years
As day tells hours. By thy clear sun
My love and fortune first did run;
But thou wilt never more appear
Folded within my hemisphere;
Since both thy light and motion
Like a fled star is fallen and gone,
And 'twixt me and my soul's dear wish
The Earth now interposèd is,
Which such a strange eclipse doth make
As ne'er was read in almanac.

   I could allow thee for a time
To darken me and my sad clime:
Were it a month, a year, or ten,
I would thy exile live till then,
And all that space my mirth adjourn,
So thou wouldst promise to return,
And putting off thy ashy shroud
At length disperse this sorrow's cloud.

   But woe is me! the longest date
Too narrow is to calculate
These empty hopes. Never shall I

Be so much blest as to descry
A glimpse of thee, till that day come
Which shall the Earth to cinders doom;
And a fierce fever must calcine
The body of this world, like thine
(My little world!). That fit of fire
Once off, our bodies shall aspire
To our souls' bliss: then we shall rise,
And view ourselves with clearer eyes
In that calm region, where no night
Can hide us from each other's sight.

   Meantime thou hast her, earth: much good
May my harm do thee. Since it stood
With heaven's will I might not call
Her longer mine, I give thee all
My short-lived right and interest
In her, whom living I loved best:
With a most free and bounteous grief
I give thee what I could not keep.
Be kind to her; and prithee look
Thou write into thy Domesday Book
Each parcel of this rarity,
Which in thy casket shrined doth lie:
See that thou make thy reck'ning straight,
And yield her back again by weight;
For thou must audit on thy trust
Each grain and atom of this dust,
As thou wilt answer him that lent,
Not gave thee, my dear monument.

   So close the ground, and about her shade
Black curtains draw: my bride is laid.

   Sleep on, my love, in thy cold bed,
Never to be disquieted.
My last good night! Thou wilt not wake
Till I thy fate shall overtake:
Till age, or grief, or sickness must
Marry my body to that dust
It so much loves, and fill the room
My heart keeps empty in thy tomb.
Stay for me there: I will not fail
To meet thee in that hollow vale.

And think not much of my delay:
I am already on the way,
And follow thee with all the speed
Desire can make, or sorrows breed.
Each minute is a short degree,
And every hour a step towards thee.
At night when I betake to rest,
Next morn I rise nearer my west
Of life, almost by eight hours' sail,
Than when sleep breathed his drowsy gale.

    Thus from the sun my bottom steers,
And my days' compass downward bears.
Nor labour I to stem the tide,
Through which to thee I swiftly glide.

    'Tis true; with shame and grief I yield:
Thou, like the van, first tookst the field,
And gotten hast the victory
In thus adventuring to die
Before me, whose more years might crave
A just precedence in the grave.
But hark! My pulse, like a soft drum,
Beats my approach, tells thee I come;
And, slow howe'er my marches be,
I shall at last sit down by thee.

    The thought of this bids me go on,
And wait my dissolution
With hope and comfort. Dear, forgive
The crime! I am content to live
Divided, with but half a heart,
Till we shall meet and never part.

HENRY KING

Sonnet 16: On His Blindness

When I consider how my light is spent,
   Ere half my days, in this dark world and wide,
   And that one talent which is death to hide
   Lodged with me useless, though my soul more bent
To serve therewith my maker, and present
   My true account, lest he returning chide,

'Doth God exact day-labour, light denied?'
I fondly ask; but patience to prevent

That murmur soon replies, 'God doth not need
    Either man's work or his own gifts; who best
    Bear his mild yoke, they serve him best, his state
Is kingly. Thousands at his bidding speed
    And post o'er land and ocean without rest:
    They also serve who only stand and wait.'

JOHN MILTON

On Time

Fly envious Time, till thou run out thy race,
Call on the lazy leaden-stepping hours,
Whose speed is but the heavy plummet's pace;
And glut thyself with what thy womb devours,
Which is no more than what is false and vain,
And merely mortal dross;
So little is our loss,
So little is thy gain.
For when as each thing bad thou hast entombed,
And last of all, thy greedy self consumed,
Then long eternity shall greet our bliss
With an individual kiss;
And joy shall overtake us as a flood,
When everything that is sincerely good
And perfectly divine,
With truth, and peace, and love shall ever shine
About the supreme throne
Of him t'whose happy-making sight alone,
When once our heavenly-guided soul shall climb,
Then all this earthly grossness quit,
Attired with stars, we shall for ever sit,
    Triumphing over death, and chance, and thee O Time.

JOHN MILTON

The Collar

I struck the board, and cried, No more.
        I will abroad.
    What? shall I ever sigh and pine?
My lines and life are free; free as the road,
    Loose as the wind, as large as store.
      Shall I be still in suit?
    Have I no harvest but a thorn
    To let me blood, and not restore
    What I have lost with cordial fruit?
      Sure there was wine
Before my sighs did dry it; there was corn
    Before my tears did drown it.
    Is the year only lost to me?
    Have I no bays to crown it?
No flowers, no garlands gay? All blasted?
      All wasted?
    Not so, my heart: but there is fruit,
    And thou hast hands.
    Recover all thy sigh-blown age
On double pleasures: leave thy cold dispute
Of what is fit, and not. Forsake thy cage,
    Thy rope of sands,
Which petty thoughts have made, and made to thee
    Good cable, to enforce and draw
    And be thy law,
    While thou didst wink and wouldst not see.
      Away; take heed,
      I will abroad,
Call in thy death's head there: tie up thy fears.
      He that forbears
    To suit and serve his need
    Deserves his load.
But as I raved and grew more fierce and wild
    At every word,
Me thoughts I heard one calling, *Child!*
    And I replied, *My Lord*.

GEORGE HERBERT

The Sinner

Lord, how I am all ague, when I seek
    What I have treasured in my memory!
    Since, if my soul make even with the week,
Each seventh note by right is due to thee.
I find there quarries of piled vanities,
    But shreds of holiness, that dare not venture
    To show their face, since cross to thy decrees:
There the circumference earth is, heav'n the centre.
In so much dregs the quintessence is small:
    The spirit and good extract of my heart
    Comes to about the many hundredth part.
Yet Lord restore thine image, hear my call:
    And though my hard heart scarce to thee can groan,
    Remember that thou once didst write in stone.

GEORGE HERBERT

from *A Masque presented at Ludlow Castle, 1634*

[COMUS]

The star that bids the shepherd fold,
Now the top of heaven doth hold,
And the gilded car of day,
His glowing axle doth allay
In the steep Atlantic stream,
And the slope sun his upward beam
Shoots against the dusky pole,
Pacing toward the other goal
Of his chamber in the east.
Meanwhile, welcome joy, and feast,
Midnight shout, and revelry,
Tipsy dance, and jollity.
Braid your locks with rosy twine
Dropping odours, dropping wine.
Rigour now is gone to bed,
And advice with scrupulous head,
Strict age, and sour severity,

With their grave saws in slumber lie.
We that are of purer fire
Imitate the starry choir,
Who in their nightly watchful spheres
Lead in swift round the months and years.
The sounds and seas with all their finny drove
Now to the moon in wavering morris move,
And on the tawny sands and shelves
Trip the pert fairies and the dapper elves;
By dimpled brook and fountain-brim
The wood-nymphs decked with daisies trim
Their merry wakes and pastimes keep:
What hath night to do with sleep?
Night hath better sweets to prove,
Venus now wakes, and wakens love.
Come let us our rites begin,
'Tis only daylight that makes sin
Which these dun shades will ne'er report;
Hail goddess of nocturnal sport,
Dark-veiled Cotytto, to whom the secret flame
Of midnight torches burns; mysterious dame
That ne'er art called but when the dragon womb
Of Stygian darkness spits her thickest gloom,
And makes one blot of all the air:
Stay thy cloudy ebon chair,
Wherein thou rid'st with Hecat', and befriend
Us thy vowed priests, till utmost end
Of all thy dues be done, and none left out,
Ere the blabbing eastern scout
The nice morn on th' Indian steep
From her cabined loophole peep,
And to the tell-tale sun descry
Our concealed solemnity.
Come, knit hands, and beat the ground,
In a light fantastic round.

JOHN MILTON

Lycidas

Yet once more, O ye laurels, and once more
Ye myrtles brown, with ivy never sere,
I come to pluck your berries harsh and crude,
And with forced fingers rude
Shatter your leaves before the mellowing year.
Bitter constraint and sad occasion dear
Compels me to disturb your season due;
For Lycidas is dead, dead ere his prime,
Young Lycidas, and hath not left his peer:
Who would not sing for Lycidas? He knew
Himself to sing, and build the lofty rhyme.
He must not float upon his watery bier
Unwept, and welter to the parching wind,
Without the meed of some melodious tear.

    Begin then, sisters of the sacred well,
That from beneath the seat of Jove doth spring;
Begin, and somewhat loudly sweep the string.
Hence with denial vain and coy excuse;
So may some gentle Muse
With lucky words favour my destined urn,
And as he passes turn,
And bid fair peace be to my sable shroud.
For we were nursed upon the self-same hill,
Fed the same flock; by fountain, shade, and rill.

    Together both, ere the high lawns appeared
Under the opening eyelids of the morn,
We drove a-field, and both together heard
What time the grey-fly winds her sultry horn,
Battening our flocks with the fresh dews of night
Oft till the star that rose, at evening, bright
Toward heaven's descent had sloped his westering wheel.
Meanwhile the rural ditties were not mute,
Tempered to the oaten flute;
Rough satyrs danced, and fauns with cloven heel
From the glad sound would not be absent long,
And old Damaetas loved to hear our song.

    But oh the heavy change, now thou art gone,
Now thou art gone, and never must return!

Thee shepherd, thee the woods and desert caves,
With wild thyme and the gadding vine o'ergrown,
And all their echoes mourn.
The willows and the hazel copses green
Shall now no more be seen,
Fanning their joyous leaves to thy soft lays.
As killing as the canker to the rose,
Or taint-worm to the weanling herds that graze,
Or frost to flowers that their gay wardrobe wear
When first the white-thorn blows:
Such, Lycidas, thy loss to shepherd's ear.

Where were ye nymphs when the remorseless deep
Closed o'er the head of your loved Lycidas?
For neither were ye playing on the steep,
Where your old bards, the famous Druids, lie,
Nor on the shaggy top of Mona high,
Nor yet where Deva spreads her wizard stream;
Ay me, I fondly dream!
Had ye been there . . . for what could that have done?
What could the Muse herself that Orpheus bore,
The Muse herself for her enchanting son
Whom universal nature did lament,
When by the rout that made the hideous roar,
His gory visage down the stream was sent,
Down the swift Hebrus to the Lesbian shore.

Alas! What boots it with uncessant care
To tend the homely slighted shepherd's trade,
And strictly meditate the thankless Muse;
Were it not better done as others use,
To sport with Amaryllis in the shade,
Or with the tangles of Neaera's hair?
Fame is the spur that the clear spirit doth raise
(That last infirmity of noble mind)
To scorn delights and live laborious days;
But the far guerdon when we hope to find,
And think to burst out into sudden blaze,
Comes the blind Fury with th' abhorrèd shears,
And slits the thin-spun life. 'But not the praise,'
Phoebus replied, and touched my trembling ears:
'Fame is no plant that grows on mortal soil,
Nor in the glistering foil

Set off to the world, nor in broad rumour lies,
But lives and spreads aloft by those pure eyes
And perfect witness of all-judging Jove;
As he pronounces lastly on each deed,
Of so much fame in heaven expect thy meed.'
   O fountain Arethuse, thou honoured flood,
Smooth-sliding Mincius, crowned with vocal reeds,
That strain I heard was of a higher mood;
But now my oat proceeds,
And listens to the herald of the sea
That came in Neptune's plea.
He asked the waves, and asked the felon winds,
What hard mishap hath doomed this gentle swain,
And questioned every gust of rugged wings
That blows from off each beakèd promontory:
They knew not of his story,
And sage Hippotades their answer brings,
That not a blast was from his dungeon strayed,
The air was calm, and on the level brine
Sleek Panope with all her sisters played.
It was that fatal and perfidious bark,
Built in the eclipse and rigged with curses dark,
That sunk so low that sacred head of thine.
   Next Camus, reverend sire, went footing slow,
His mantle hairy, and his bonnet sedge,
Inwrought with figures dim, and on the edge
Like to that sanguine flower inscribed with woe.
'Ah; who hath reft,' quoth he, 'my dearest pledge?'
Last came, and last did go,
The pilot of the Galilean lake;
Two massy keys he bore of metals twain,
(The golden opes, the iron shuts amain).
He shook his mitred locks, and stern bespake,
'How well could I have spared for thee, young swain,
Enow of such as for their bellies' sake
Creep and intrude and climb into the fold!
Of other care they little reckoning make
Than how to scramble at the shearer's feast,
And shove away the worthy bidden guest;
Blind mouths! that scarce themselves know how to hold
A sheep-hook, or have learned aught else the least

That to the faithful herdman's art belongs!
What recks it them? What need they? They are sped;
And when they list, their lean and flashy songs
Grate on their scrannel pipes of wretched straw,
The hungry sheep look up, and are not fed,
But swollen with wind and the rank mist they draw
Rot inwardly, and foul contagion spread;
Besides what the grim wolf with privy paw
Daily devours apace, and nothing said;
But that two-handed engine at the door
Stands ready to smite once, and smite no more.'
    Return Alpheus, the dread voice is past
That shrunk thy streams; return Sicilian Muse,
And call the vales, and bid them hither cast
Their bells and flowrets of a thousand hues.
Ye valleys low where the mild whispers use
Of shades and wanton winds and gushing brooks,
On whose fresh lap the swart star sparely looks,
Throw hither all your quaint enamelled eyes,
That on the green turf suck the honied showers,
And purple all the ground with vernal flowers.
Bring the rathe primrose that forsaken dies,
The tufted crow-toe and pale jessamine,
The white pink and the pansy freaked with jet,
The glowing violet,
The musk-rose and the well-attired woodbine,
With cowslips wan that hang the pensive head,
And every flower that sad embroidery wears:
Bid amaranthus all his beauty shed,
And daffadillies fill their cups with tears,
To strew the laureate hearse where Lycid lies.
For so to interpose a little ease
Let our frail thoughts dally with false surmise.
Ay me! Whilst thee the shores and sounding seas
Wash far away, where'er thy bones are hurled:
Whether beyond the stormy Hebrides,
Where thou perhaps under the whelming tide
Visitst the bottom of the monstrous world;
Or whether thou, to our moist vows denied,
Sleepst by the fable of Bellerus old,
Where the great vision of the guarded mount

Looks toward Namancos and Bayona's hold;
Look homeward angel now, and melt with ruth.
And, O ye dolphins, waft the hapless youth.
  Weep no more, woeful shepherds weep no more,
For Lycidas your sorrow is not dead,
Sunk though he be beneath the watery floor;
So sinks the day-star in the ocean bed,
And yet anon repairs his drooping head,
And tricks his beams, and with new spangled ore
Flames in the forehead of the morning sky:
So Lycidas sunk low, but mounted high,
Through the dear might of him that walked the waves;
Where other groves, and other streams along,
With nectar pure his oozy locks he laves,
And hears the unexpressive nuptial song,
In the blest kingdoms meek of joy and love.
There entertain him all the saints above,
In solemn troops and sweet societies
That sing, and singing in their glory move,
And wipe the tears for ever from his eyes.
Now Lycidas the shepherds weep no more;
Henceforth thou art the genius of the shore,
In thy large recompense, and shalt be good
To all that wander in that perilous flood.
  Thus sang the uncouth swain to the oaks and rills;
While the still morn went out with sandals grey,
He touched the tender stops of various quills,
With eager thought warbling his Doric lay:
And now the sun had stretched out all the hills,
And now was dropped into the western bay;
At last he rose, and twitched his mantle blue:
Tomorrow to fresh woods, and pastures new.

JOHN MILTON

On Shakespeare

What needs my Shakespeare for his honoured bones
The labour of an age in piled stones
Or that his hallowed relics should be hid
Under a starry-pointing pyramid?

Dear son of memory, great heir of fame,
What needst thou such weak witness of thy name?
Thou in our wonder and astonishment
Hast built thyself a livelong monument.
For whilst to th'shame of slow-endeavouring art,
Thy easy numbers flow, and that each heart
Hath from the leaves of thy unvalued book
Those Delphic lines with deep impression took,
Then thou our fancy of itself bereaving,
Dost make us marble with too much conceiving;
And so sepulchered in such pomp dost lie,
That kings for such a tomb would wish to die.

JOHN MILTON

Sonnet 19

Methought I saw my late espousèd saint
    Brought to me like Alcestis from the grave,
    Whom Jove's great son to her glad husband gave,
    Rescued from death by force though pale and faint.
Mine as whom washed from spot of childbed taint
    Purification in the old Law did save,
    And such as yet once more I trust to have
    Full sight of her in heaven without restraint,
Came vested all in white, pure as her mind:
    Her face was veiled, yet to my fancied sight
    Love, sweetness, goodness in her person shined
So clear as in no face with more delight.
But oh as to embrace me she inclined
I waked, she fled, and day brought back my night.

JOHN MILTON

On the Morning of Christ's Nativity

This is the month, and this the happy morn,
Wherein the Son of Heaven's eternal King,
Of wedded Maid and Virgin Mother Born,
Our great redemption from above did bring;
For so the holy sages once did sing,

That he our deadly forfeit should release,
And with his Father work us a perpetual peace.

That glorious form, that light unsufferable,
And that far-beaming blaze of majesty,
Wherewith he wont at Heaven's high council-table
To sit the midst of Trinal Unity,
He laid aside; and here with us to be,
    Forsook the courts of everlasting day,
And chose with us a darksome house of mortal clay.

Say, Heavenly Muse, shall not thy sacred vein
Afford a present to the infant God?
Hast thou no verse, no hymn, or solemn strain,
To welcome him to this his new abode,
Now while the heaven, by the sun's team untrod,
    Hath took no print of the approaching light,
And all the spangled host keep watch in squadrons bright?

See how from upon the eastern road
The star-led wizards haste with odors sweet!
O run, prevent them with thy humble ode,
And lay it lowly at his blessed feet;
Have thou the honor first thy Lord to greet,
    And join thy voice unto the angel choir,
From out his secret altar touched with hallowed fire.

THE HYMN

It was the winter wild
While the Heaven-born child
    All meanly wrapped in the rude manger lies;
Nature in awe to him
Had doffed her gaudy trim,
    With her great Master so to sympathize;
It was no season then for her
To wanton with the sun, her lusty paramour.

Only with speeches fair
She woos the gentle air
    To hide her guilty front with innocent snow,
And on her naked shame,
Pollute with sinful blame,

The saintly veil of maiden white to throw,
Confounded, that her Maker's eyes
Should look so near upon her foul deformities.

But he her fears to cease,
Sent down the meek-eyed Peace;
   She, crowned with olive green, came softly sliding
Down through the turning sphere,
His ready harbinger,
   With turtle wing the amorous clouds dividing,
And waving wide her myrtle wand,
She strikes a universal peace through sea and land.

No war or battle's sound
Was heard the world around:
   The idle spear and shield were high uphung;
The hooked chariot stood
Unstained with hostile blood;
   The trumpet spake not to the armed throng;
And kings sat still with awful eye,
As if they surely knew their sovran Lord was by.

But peaceful was the night
Wherein the Prince of Light
   His reign of peace upon the earth began:
The winds with wonder whist,
Smoothly the waters kissed,
   Whispering new joys to the mild ocëan,
Who now hath quite forgot to rave,
While birds of calm sit brooding on the charmed wave.

The stars with deep amaze
Stand fixed in steadfast gaze,
   Bending one way their precious influence,
And will not take their flight
For all the morning light,
   Or Lucifer that often warned them thence;
But in their glimmering orbs did glow,
Until their Lord himself bespake, and bid them go.

And though the shady gloom
Had given day her room,
   The sun himself withheld his wonted speed,
And hid his head for shame,

As his inferior flame
　　The new-enlightened world no more should need;
He saw a greater sun appear
Than his bright throne or burning axletree could bear.

The shepherds on the lawn,
Or ere the point of dawn,
　　Sat simply chatting in a rustic row;
Full little thought they than
That the mighty Pan
　　Was kindly come to live with them below;
Perhaps their loves, or else their sheep,
Was all that did their silly thoughts so busy keep.

When such music sweet
Their hearts and ears did greet,
　　As never was by mortal finger strook,
Divinely warbled voice
Answering the stringed noise,
　　As all their souls in blissful rapture took;
The air, such pleasure loth to lose,
With thousand echoes still prolongs each heavenly close.

Nature that heard such sound
Beneath the hollow round
　　Of Cynthia's seat, the airy region thrilling,
Now was almost won
To think her part was done,
　　And that her reign had here its last fulfilling;
She knew such harmony alone
Could hold all Heaven and Earth in happier union.

At last surrounds their sight
A globe of circular light,
　　That with long beams the shame-faced Night arrayed;
The helmed Cherubim
And sworded Seraphim
　　Are seen in glittering ranks with wings displayed,
Harping in loud and solemn choir,
With unexpressive notes to Heaven's new-born Heir.

Such music (as 'tis said)
Before was never made,
　　But when of old the sons of morning sung,

While the Creator great
His constellations set,
   And the well-balanced world on hinges hung,
And cast the dark foundations deep,
And bid the weltering waves their oozy channel keep.

Ring out, ye crystal spheres,
Once bless our human ears
   (If ye have power to touch our senses so),
And let your silver chime
Move in melodious time,
   And let the bass of Heaven's deep organ blow;
And with your ninefold harmony
Make up full consort to the angelic symphony.

For if such holy song
Enwrap our fancy long,
   Time will run back and fetch the age of gold,
And speckled Vanity
Will sicken soon and die,
   And leprous Sin will melt from earthly mold,
And Hell itself will pass away,
And leave her dolorous mansions to the peering day.

Yea, Truth and Justice then
Will down return to men,
   Orbed in a rainbow; and like glories wearing,
Mercy will sit between,
Throned in celestial sheen,
   With radiant feet the tissued clouds down steering;
And Heaven, as at some festival,
Will open wide the gates of her high palace hall.

But wisest Fate says no,
This must not yet be so;
   The Babe lies yet in smiling infancy,
That on the bitter cross
Must redeem our loss,
   So both himself and us to glorify;
Yet first to those ychained in sleep,
The wakeful trump of doom must thunder through the deep,

With such a horrid clang
As on Mount Sinai rang
    While the red fire and smoldering clouds outbrake:
The aged Earth aghast
With terror of that blast,
    Shall from the surface to the centre shake,
When at the world's last session
The dreadful Judge in middle air shall spread his throne.

And then at last our bliss
Full and perfect is,
    But now begins; for from this happy day
The old Dragon under ground,
In straiter limits bound,
    Not half so far casts his usurped sway,
And, wroth to see his kingdom fail,
Swinges the scaly horror of his folded tail.

The oracles are dumb,
No voice or hideous hum
    Runs through the arched roof in words deceiving.
Apollo from his shrine
Can no more divine,
    With hollow shriek the steep of Delphos leaving.
No nightly trance or breathed spell
Inspires the pale-eyed priest from the prophetic cell.

The lonely mountains o'er,
And the resounding shore,
    A voice of weeping heard, and loud lament;
From haunted spring and dale,
Edged with poplar pale,
    The parting Genius is with sighing sent;
With flower-inwoven tresses torn
The nymphs in twilight shade of tangled thickets mourn.

In consecrated earth,
And on the holy hearth,
    The Lars and Lemures moan with midnight plaint;
In urns and altars round,
A drear and dying sound
    Affrights the flamens at their service quaint;

And the chill marble seems to sweat,
While each peculiar power forgoes his wonted seat.

Peor and Baalim
Forsake their temples dim,
   With that twice-battered god of Palestine;
And mooned Ashtaroth,
Heaven's queen and mother both,
   Now sits not girt with tapers' holy shine;
The Libyc Hammon shrinks his horn,
In vain the Tyrian maids their wounded Thammuz mourn.

And sullen Moloch, fled,
Hath left in shadows dread
   His burning idol all of blackest hue;
In vain with cymbals' ring
They call the grisly king,
   In dismal dance about the furnace blue;
The brutish gods of Nile as fast,
Isis and Orus, and the dog Anubis, haste.

Nor is Osiris seen
In Memphian grove or green,
   Trampling the unshowered grass with lowings loud;
Nor can he be at rest
Within his sacred chest,
   Nought but profoundest Hell can be his shroud;
In vain with timbreled anthems dark
The sable-stoled sorcerers bear his worshiped ark.

He feels from Juda's land
The dreaded Infant's hand,
   The rays of Bethlehem blind his dusky eyn;
Nor all the gods beside
Longer dare abide,
   Not Typhon huge ending in snaky twine:
Our Babe, to show his Godhead true,
Can in his swaddling bands control the damned crew.

So when the sun in bed,
Curtained with cloudy red,
   Pillows his chin upon an orient wave,
The flocking shadows pale
Troop to the infernal jail;

Each fettered ghost slips to his several grave,
And the yellow-skirted fays
Fly after the night-steeds, leaving their moon-loved maze.

But see, the Virgin blest
Hath laid her Babe to rest.
    Time is our tedious song should here have ending;
Heaven's youngest-teemed star
Hath fixed her polished car,
    Her sleeping Lord with handmaid lamp attending;
And all about the courtly stable
Bright-harnessed angels sit in order serviceable.

JOHN MILTON

The Unquiet Grave

'The wind doth blow to-day, my love,
    And a few small drops of rain;
I never had but one true-love;
    In cold grave she was lain.

'I'll do as much for my true-love
    As any young man may;
I'll sit and mourn all at her grave
    For a twelvemonth and a day.'

The twelvemonth and a day being up,
    The dead began to speak:
'Oh who sits weeping on my grave,
    And will not let me sleep?' –

''Tis I, my love, sits on your grave,
    And will not let you sleep;
For I crave one kiss of your clay-cold lips,
    And that is all I seek.' –

'You crave one kiss of my clay-cold lips;
    But my breath smells earthy strong;
If you have one kiss of my clay-cold lips,
    Your time will not be long.

''Tis down in yonder garden green,
    Love, where we used to walk,

The finest flower that ere was seen
  Is wither'd to a stalk.

'The stalk is wither'd dry, my love,
  So will our hearts decay;
So make yourself content, my love,
  Till God calls you away.'

ANON.

The Death and Burial of Cock Robbin

Here lies Cock Robbin dead and cold:
  His end this book will soon unfold!

'Who did kill Cock Robbin?'
'I,' said the sparrow, 'with my bow and arrow,
I did kill Cock Robbin.'

'Who did see him die?'
'I,' said the fly, 'with my little eye,
And I did see him die.'

'And who catch'd his blood?'
'I,' said the fish, 'with my little dish,
And I catch'd his blood.'

'And who did make his shroud?'
'I,' said the beetle, 'with my little needle,
And I did make his shroud.'

'Who'll dig his grave?'
'I,' said the owl,
'With my spade and show'l,
And I'll dig his grave.'

'Who'll be the parson?'
'I,' said the rook,
'With my little book,
And I'll be the parson.'

'Who'll be the clerk?'
'I,' said the lark,
'If 'tis not in the dark,
And I'll be the clerk.'

'Who'll carry him to the grave?'
'I,' said the kite,
'If 'tis not in the night,
And I'll carry him to the grave.'

'Who'll carry the link?'
'I,' said the linnet,
'I'll fetch it in a minute,
And I'll carry the link.'

'Who'll be chief mourner?'
'I,' said the swan,
'I'm sorry he's gone,
And I'll be chief mourner.'

'Who'll bear the pall?'
'We,' said the wren,
Both the cock and the hen,
'And we'll bear the pall.'

'Who'll run before?'
'I,' said the deer,
'I run fast for fear,
And I'll run before.'

'Who'll sing a psalm?'
'I,' said the thrush,
As she sat in a bush,
'And I'll sing a psalm.'

'Who'll throw in the dirt?'
'I,' said the fox,
'Though I steal hens and cocks,
I'll throw in the dirt.'

'And who'll toll the bell?'
'I,' said the bull,
'Because I can pull,
And so, Cock Robbin, farewell!'

All the birds of the air
Fell to sighing and sobbing,
When they heard the bell toll
For poor Cock Robbin.

ANON.

Sir Patrick Spens

THE SAILING

The king sits in Dunfermline town
    Drinking the blude-red wine;
'O whare will I get a skeely skipper
    To sail this new ship o' mine?'

O up and spak an eldern knight,
    Sat at the king's right knee:
'Sir Patrick Spens is the best sailor
    That ever sail'd the sea.'

Our king has written a braid letter,
    And seal'd it with his hand,
And sent it to Sir Patrick Spens,
    Was walking on the strand.

'To Noroway, to Noroway,
    To Noroway o'er the faem;
The king's daughter o' Noroway,
    'Tis thou must bring her hame.'

The first word that Sir Patrick read
    So loud, loud laugh'd he;
The neist word that Sir Patrick read
    The tear blinded his e'e.

'O wha is this has done this deed
    And tauld the king o' me,
To send us out, at this time o' year,
    To sail upon the sea?

'Be it wind, be it weet, be it hail, be it sleet,
    Our ship must sail the faem;
The king's daughter o' Noroway,
    'Tis we must fetch her hame.'

They hoysed their sails on Monenday morn
    Wi' a' the speed they may;

They hae landed in Noroway
   Upon a Wodensday.

THE RETURN

'Mak ready, mak ready, my merry men a'!
   Our gude ship sails the morn.' –
'Now ever alack, my master dear,
   I fear a deadly storm.

'I saw the new moon late yestreen
   Wi' the auld moon in her arm;
And if we gang to sea, master,
   I fear we'll come to harm.'

They hadna sail'd a league, a league,
   A league but barely three,
When the lift grew dark, and the wind blew loud,
   And gurly grew the sea.

The ankers brak, and the topmast lap,
   It was sic a deadly storm:
And the waves cam owre the broken ship
   Till a' her sides were torn.

'O where will I get a gude sailor
   To tak' my helm in hand,
Till I get up to the tall topmast
   To see if I can spy land?' –

'O here am I, a sailor gude,
   To tak' the helm in hand,
Till you go up to the tall topmast,
   But I fear you'll ne'er spy land.'

He hadna gane a step, a step,
   A step but barely ane,
When a bolt flew out of our goodly ship,
   And the saut sea it came in.

'Go fetch a web o' the silken claith,
   Another o' the twine,
And wap them into our ship's side,
   And let nae the sea come in.'

They fetch'd a web o' the silken claith,
    Another o' the twine,
And they wapp'd them round that gude ship's side,
    But still the sea came in.

O laith, laith were our gude Scots lords
    To wet their cork-heel'd shoon;
But lang or a' the play was play'd
    They wat their hats aboon.

And mony was the feather bed
    That flatter'd on the faem;
And mony was the gude lord's son
    That never mair cam hame.

O lang, lang may the ladies sit,
    Wi' their fans into their hand,
Before they see Sir Patrick Spens
    Come sailing to the strand!

And lang, lang may the maidens sit
    Wi' their gowd kames in their hair,
A-waiting for their ain dear loves!
    For them they'll see nae mair.

Half-owre, half-owre to Aberdour,
    'Tis fifty fathoms deep;
And there lies gude Sir Patrick Spens,
    Wi' the Scots lords at his feet!

ANON.

Evening Quatrains

The day's grown old, the fainting sun
Has but a little way to run;
And yet his steeds, with all his skill,
Scarce lug the chariot down the hill.

With labour spent and thirst oppressed,
Whilst they strain hard to gain the west,
From fetlocks hot drops melted light,
Which turn to meteors in the night.

The shadows now so long do grow
That brambles like tall cedars show,
Molehills seem mountains, and the ant
Appears a monstrous elephant.

A very little little flock
Shades thrice the ground that it would stock;
Whilst the small stripling following them
Appears a mighty Polypheme.

These being brought into the fold,
And by the thrifty master told,
He thinks his wages are well paid,
Since none are either lost or strayed.

Now lowing herds are each-where heard;
Chains rattle in the villains' yard;
The cart's on tail set down to rest,
Bearing on high the cuckold's crest.

The hedge is stripped, the clothes brought in,
Nought's left without should be within;
The bees are hived, and hum their charm;
Whilst every house does seem a swarm.

The cock now to the roost is prest
For he must call up all the rest;
The sow's fast pegged within the sty,
To still her squeaking progeny.

Each one has had his supping mess,
The cheese is put into the press,
The pans and bowls clean scalded all,
Reared up against the milk-house wall.

And now on benches all are sat
In the cool air to sit and chat,
Till Phoebus, dipping in the west,
Shall lead the world the way to rest.

CHARLES COTTON

The Definition of Love

My love is of a birth as rare
As 'tis for object strange and high:
It was begotten by despair
Upon impossibility.

Magnanimous despair alone
Could show me so divine a thing,
Where feeble hope could ne'er have flown
But vainly flapped its tinsel wing.

And yet I quickly might arrive
Where my extended soul is fixed;
But fate does iron wedges drive,
And always crowds itself betwixt.

For fate with jealous eye does see
Two perfect loves, nor lets them close:
Their union would her ruin be,
And her tyrannic power depose.

And therfore her decrees of steel
Us as the distant poles have placed,
(Though love's whole world on us doth wheel)
Not by themselves to be embraced,

Unless the giddy heaven fall,
And Earth some new convulsion tear;
And, us to join, the world should all
Be clamped into a planisphere.

As lines so loves oblique may well
Themselves in every angle greet:
But ours so truly parallel,
Though infinite, can never meet.

Therefore the love which us doth bind
But fate so enviously debars
Is the conjunction of the mind
And opposition of the stars.

ANDREW MARVELL

To His Coy Mistress

Had we but world enough, and time,
This coyness, Lady, were no crime.
We would sit down, and think which way
To walk, and pass our long love's day.

Thou by the Indian Ganges' side
Shouldst rubies find: I by the tide
Of Humber would complain. I would
Love you ten years before the Flood:
And you should, if you please, refuse
Till the conversion of the Jews.
My vegetable love should grow
Vaster than empires, and more slow.
An hundred years should go to praise
Thine eyes, and on thy forehead gaze.
Two hundred to adore each breast;
But thirty thousand to the rest.
An age at least to every part,
And the last age should show your heart:
For, Lady, you deserve this state;
Nor would I love at lower rate.
    But at my back I always hear
Time's wingèd chariot hurrying near;
And yonder all before us lie
Deserts of vast eternity.
Thy beauty shall no more be found;
Nor, in thy marble vault, shall sound
My echoing song: then worms shall try
That long-preserved virginity:
And your quaint honour turn to dust;
And into ashes all my lust.
The grave's a fine and private place,
But none, I think, do there embrace.
    Now, therefore, while the youthful glue
Sits on thy skin like morning dew,
And while thy willing soul transpires
At every pore with instant fires,
Now let us sport us while we may;

And now, like amorous birds of prey,
Rather at once our time devour,
Than languish in his slow-chapped power.
Let us roll all our strength, and all
Our sweetness, up into one ball:
And tear our pleasures with rough strife
Thorough the iron grates of life.

Thus, though we cannot make our sun
Stand still, yet we will make him run.

ANDREW MARVELL

On a Drop of Dew

See how the orient dew,
Shed from the bosom of the morn
    Into the blowing roses,
Yet careless of its mansion new,
For the clear region where 'twas born
    Round in itself incloses:
    And in its little globe's extent,
Frames as it can its native element.
    How it the purple flow'r does slight,
        Scarce touching where it lies,
    But gazing back upon the skies,
        Shines with a mournful light,
            Like its own tear,
Because so long divided from the sphere.
    Restless it rolls and unsecure,
        Trembling lest it grow impure,
    Till the warm sun pity its pain,
And to the skies exhale it back again.
        So the soul, that drop, that ray
Of the clear fountain of eternal day,
Could it within the human flow'r be seen,
        Remembering still its former height,
        Shuns the sweet leaves and blossoms green,
        And recollecting its own light,
Does, in its pure and circling thoughts, express
The greater heaven in an heaven less.

In how coy a figure wound,
Every way it turns away:
So the world excluding round,
Yet receiving in the day,
Dark beneath, but bright above,
Here disdaining, there in love.
How loose and easy hence to go,
How girt and ready to ascend,
Moving but on a point below,
It all about does upwards bend.
Such did the manna's sacred dew distill,
White and entire, though congealed and chill,
Congealed on earth: but does, dissolving, run
Into the glories of th' almighty sun.

ANDREW MARVELL

Tam Lin

'O I forbid you, maidens a',
    That wear gowd on your hair,
To come or gae by Carterhaugh,
    For young Tam Lin is there.

'For even about that knight's middle
    O' siller bells are nine;
And nae maid comes to Carterhaugh
    And a maid returns again.'

Fair Janet sat in her bonny bower,
    Sewing her silken seam,
And wish'd to be in Carterhaugh
    Amang the leaves sae green.

She's lat her seam fa' to her feet,
    The needle to her tae,
And she's awa' to Carterhaugh
    As fast as she could gae.

And she has kilted her green kirtle
    A little abune her knee;
And she has braided her yellow hair
    A little abune her bree;

And she has gaen for Carterhaugh
  As fast as she can hie.

She hadna pu'd a rose, a rose,
  A rose but barly ane,
When up and started young Tam Lin;
  Says, 'Ladye, let alane.

'What gars ye pu' the rose, Janet?
  What gars ye break the tree?
What gars ye come to Carterhaugh
  Without the leave o' me?'

'Weel may I pu' the rose,' she says,
  'And ask no leave at thee;
For Carterhaugh it is my ain,
  My daddy gave it me.'

He's ta'en her by the milk-white hand,
  And by the grass-green sleeve,
He's led her to the fairy ground
  At her he ask'd nae leave.

Janet has kilted her green kirtle
  A little abune her knee,
And she has snooded her yellow hair
  A little abune her bree,
And she is to her father's ha'
  As fast as she can hie.

But when she came to her father's ha',
  She look'd sae wan and pale,
They thought the lady had gotten a fright,
  Or with sickness she did ail.

Four and twenty ladies fair
  Were playing at the ba',
And out then came fair Janet
  Ance the flower amang them a'.

Four and twenty ladies fair
  Were playing at the chess,
And out then came fair Janet
  As green as onie glass.

Out then spak' an auld grey knight
  'Lay owre the Castle wa',
And say, 'Alas, fair Janet!
  For thee we'll be blamèd a'.'

'Hauld your tongue, ye auld-faced knight,
  Some ill death may ye die!
Father my bairn on whom I will,
  I'll father nane on thee.

'O if my love were an earthly knight,
  As he is an elfin gay,
I wadna gie my ain true-love
  For nae laird that ye hae.

'The steed that my true-love rides on
  Is fleeter nor the wind;
Wi' siller he is shod before,
  Wi' burning gold behind.'

Out then spak' her brither dear –
  He meant to do her harm:
'There grows an herb in Carterhaugh
  Will twine you an' the bairn.'

Janet has kilted her green kirtle
  A little abune her knee,
And she has snooded her yellow hair
  A little abune her bree,
And she's awa' to Carterhaugh
  As fast as she can hie.

She hadna pu'd a leaf, a leaf,
  A leaf but only twae,
When up and started young Tam Lin,
  Says, 'Ladye, thou's pu' nae mae.

'How dar' ye pu' a leaf?' he says
'How dar' ye break the tree?
How dar' ye scathe my babe,' he says,
  'That's between you and me?'

'O tell me, tell me, Tam,' she says,
  'For His sake that died on tree,
If ye were ever in holy chapel
  Or sain'd in Christentie?'

'The truth I'll tell to thee, Janet,
　　Ae word I winna lee;
A knight me got, and a lady me bore,
　　As well as they did thee.

'Roxburgh he was my grandfather,
　　Took me with him to bide;
And ance it fell upon a day,
　　As hunting I did ride,

'There came a wind out o' the north,
　　A sharp wind an' a snell,
A dead sleep it came over me
　　And frae my horse I fell;
And the Queen o' Fairies she took me
　　In yon green hill to dwell.

'And pleasant is the fairy land
　　For those that in it dwell,
But ay at end of seven years
　　They pay a teind to hell;
I am sae fair and fu' o' flesh
　　I'm fear'd 'twill be mysell.

'But the night is Hallowe'en, Janet,
　　The morn is Hallowday;
Then win me, win me, an ye will,
　　For weel I wat ye may.

'The night it is gude Hallowe'en,
　　The fairy folk do ride,
And they that wad their true-love win,
　　At Miles Cross they maun bide.' –

'But how should I you ken, Tam Lin,
　　How should I borrow you,
Amang a pack of uncouth knights
　　The like I never saw?' –

'You'll do you down to Miles Cross
　　Between twel' hours and ane,
And fill your hands o' the holy water
　　And cast your compass roun'.

'The first company that passes by,
    Say na, and let them gae;
The neist company that passes by,
    Say na, and do right sae;
The third company that passes by,
    Then I'll be ane o' thae.

'O first let pass the black, ladye,
    And syne let pass the brown;
But quickly run to the milk-white steed,
    Pu' ye his rider down.

'For some ride on the black, ladye,
    And some ride on the brown;
But I ride on a milk-white steed,
    A gowd star on my crown:
Because I was an earthly knight
    They gie me that renown.

'My right hand will be gloved, ladye,
    My left hand will be bare,
And thae's the tokens I gie thee:
    Nae doubt I will be there.

'Ye'll tak' my horse then by the head
    And let the bridle fa';
The Queen o' Elfin she'll cry out
    "True Tam Lin he's awa'!"

'They'll turn me in your arms, ladye,
    An aske but and a snake;
But hauld me fast, let me na gae,
    To be your warldis make.

'They'll turn me in your arms, ladye
    But and a deer so wild;
But hauld me fast, let me na gae,
    The father o' your child.

'They'll shape me in your arms, ladye,
    A hot iron at the fire;
But hauld me fast, let me na go,
    To be your heart's desire.

'They'll shape me last in your arms, Janet,
    A mother-naked man;
Cast your green mantle over me,
    And sae will I be won.'

Janet has kilted her green kirtle
    A little abune the knee;
And she has snooded her yellow hair
    A little abune her bree,
And she is on to Miles Cross
    As fast as she can hie.

About the dead hour o' the night
    She heard the bridles ring;
And Janet was as glad at that;
    As any earthly thing.

And first gaed by the black, black steed,
    And syne gaed by the brown;
But fast she gript the milk-white steed
    And pu'd the rider down.

She's pu'd him frae the milk-white steed,
    An' loot the bridle fa',
And up there rase an eldritch cry,
    'True Tam Lin he's awa'!'

They shaped him in her arms twa
    An aske but and a snake;
But aye she grips and hau'ds him fast
    To be her warldis make.

They shaped him in her arms twa
    But and a deer sae wild;
But aye she grips and hau'ds him fast,
    The father o' her child.

They shaped him in her arms twa
    A hot iron at the fire;
But aye she grips and hau'ds him fast
    To be her heart's desire.

They shaped him in her arms at last
    A mother-naked man;
She cast her mantle over him,
    And sae her love she wan.

Up then spak' the Queen o' Fairies,
   Out o' a bush o' broom,
'She that has borrow'd young Tam Lin
   Has gotten a stately groom.'

Out then spak' the Queen o' Fairies,
   And an angry woman was she,
'She's ta'en awa' the bonniest knight
   In a' my companie!

'But what I ken this night, Tam Lin,
   Gin I had kent yestreen,
I wad ta'en out thy heart o' flesh,
   And put in a heart o' stane.

'And adieu, Tam Lin! But gin I had kent
   A ladye wad borrow'd thee,
I wad ta'en out thy twa grey e'en
   Put in twa e'en o' tree.

'And had I the wit yestreen, yestreen,
   That I have coft this day,
I'd paid my teind seven times to hell
   Ere you had been won away!'

ANON.

The Mower to the Glo-Worms

Ye living lamps, by whose dear light
The nightingale does sit so late,
And studying all the summer-night,
Her matchless songs does meditate;

Ye country comets, that portend
No war, nor princes funeral,
Shining unto no higher end
Than to presage the grasses fall;

Ye Glow-worms, whose officious flame
To wandring mowers shows the way,
That in the night have lost their aim,
And after foolish fires do stray;

Your courteous lights in vain you waste,
Since Juliana here is come,
For she my mind hath so displac'd
That I shall never find my home.

ANDREW MARVELL

The Garden

How vainly men themselves amaze
To win the palm, the oak, or bays,
And their uncessant labours see
Crowned from some single herb or tree,
Whose short and narrow vergèd shade
Does prudently their toils upbraid,
While all flow'rs and all trees do close
To weave the garlands of repose.

Fair quiet, have I found thee here,
And innocence thy sister dear!
Mistaken long, I sought you then
In busy companies of men.
Your sacred plants, if here below,
Only among the plants will grow.
Society is all but rude,
To this delicious solitude.

No white nor red was ever seen
So am'rous as this lovely green.
Fond lovers, cruel as their flame,
Cut in these trees their mistress' name.
Little alas, they know, or heed,
How far these beauties hers exceed!
Fair trees! wheres'e'er your barks I wound,
No name shall but your own be found.

When we have run our passion's heat,
Love hither makes his best retreat.
The gods, that mortal beauty chase,
Still in a tree did end their race.
Apollo hunted Daphne so,

Only that she might laurel grow:
And Pan did after Syrinx speed,
Not as a nymph, but for a reed.

What wondrous life in this I lead!
Ripe apples drop about my head;
The luscious clusters of the vine
Upon my mouth do crush their wine;
The nectarine and curious peach
Into my hands themselves do reach;
Stumbling on melons, as I pass,
Ensnared with flowers, I fall on grass.

Meanwhile the mind, from pleasures less,
Withdraws into its happiness:
The mind, that ocean where each kind
Does straight its own resemblance find;
Yet it creates, transcending these,
Far other worlds, and other seas,
Annihilating all that's made
To a green thought in a green shade.

Here at the fountain's sliding foot,
Or at some fruit-tree's mossy root,
Casting the body's vest aside,
My soul into the boughs does glide.
There like a bird it sits, and sings,
Then whets, and combs its silver wings;
And, till prepared for longer flight,
Waves in its plumes the various light.

Such was that happy garden-state,
While man there walked without a mate:
After a place so pure, and sweet,
What other help could yet be meet!
But 'twas beyond a mortal's share
To wander solitary there:
Two paradises 'twere in one
To live in paradise alone.

How well the skilful gardener drew
Of flowers and herbs this dial new;
Where from above the milder sun

Does through a fragrant zodiac run;
And, as it works, the industrious bee
Computes its time as well as we.
How could such sweet and wholesome hours
Be reckoned but with herbs and flowers!

ANDREW MARVELL

Peace

My soul, there is a country
   Far beyond the stars,
Where stands a winged sentry
   All skilful in the wars,
There above noise, and danger
   Sweet peace sits crowned with smiles,
And one born in a manger
   Commands the beauteous files,
He is thy gracious friend,
   And (O my soul awake!)
Did in pure love descend
   To die here for thy sake,
If thou canst get but thither,
   There grows the flower of peace,
The rose that cannot wither,
   Thy fortress, and thy ease;
Leave then thy foolish ranges;
   For none can thee secure,
But one, who never changes,
   Thy God, thy life, thy cure.

HENRY VAUGHAN

On a Cock at Rochester

Thou cursèd cock, with thy perpetual noise,
Mayst thou be capon made, and lose thy voice,
Or on a dunghill mayst thou spend thy blood,
And vermin prey upon thy craven brood;
May rivals tread thy hens before thy face,
Then with redoubled courage give thee chase;

90

Mayst thou be punished for St Peter's crime,
And on Shrove Tuesday perish in thy prime;
May thy bruised carcass be some beggar's feast,
Thou first and worst disturber of man's rest.

SIR CHARLES SEDLEY

The Water-fall

With what deep murmurs through time's silent stealth
Doth thy transparent, cool and watery wealth
    Here flowing fall,
    And chide, and call,
As if his liquid, loose retinue stayed
Ling'ring and were of this steep place afraid,
    The common pass
    Where, clear as glass,
    All must descend
    Not to an end:
But quickened by this deep and rocky grave,
Rise to a longer course more bright and brave.
Dear stream! dear bank, where often I
Have sat, and pleased my pensive eye,
Why, since each drop of thy quick store
Runs thither, whence it flowed before,
Should poor souls fear a shade or night,
Who came (sure) from a sea of light?
Or since those drops are all sent back
So sure to thee, that none doth lack,
Why should frail flesh doubt any more
That what God takes, he'll not restore?
O useful element and clear!
My sacred wash and cleanser here,
My first consigner unto those
Fountains of life, where the Lamb goes?
What sublime truths, and wholesome themes,
Lodge in thy mystical, deep streams!
Such as dull man can never find
Unless that Spirit lead his mind,
Which first upon thy face did move,
And hatched all with his quickening love.

91

As this loud brook's incessant fall
In streaming rings restagnates all,
Which reach by course the bank, and then
Are no more seen, just so pass men.
O my invisible estate,
My glorious liberty, still late!
Thou art the channel my soul seeks,
Not this with cataracts and creeks.

HENRY VAUGHAN

Of Many Worlds in This World

Just like unto a nest of boxes round,
Degrees of sizes within each box are found,
So in this world may many worlds more be,
Thinner, and less, and less still by degree;
Although they are not subject to our sense,
A world may be no bigger than twopence.
Nature is curious, and such work may make
That our dull sense can never find, but scape.
For creatures small as atoms may be there,
If every atom a creature's figure bear.
If four atoms a world can make, then see
What several worlds might in an ear-ring be.
For millions of these atoms may be in
The head of one small, little, single pin.
And if thus small, then ladies well may wear
A world of worlds as pendents in each ear.

MARGARET CAVENDISH, DUCHESS OF NEWCASTLE

'They are all gone into the world of light!'

They are all gone into the world of light!
    And I alone sit ling'ring here;
Their very memory is fair and bright,
    And my sad thoughts doth clear.

It glows and glitters in my cloudy breast
    Like stars upon some gloomy grove,
Or those faint beams in which this hill is dressed,
      After the sun's remove.

I see them walking in an air of glory,
    Whose light doth trample on my days:
My days, which are at best but dull and hoary,
      Mere glimmering and decays.

O holy hope! and high humility,
    High as the heavens above!
These are your walks, and you have showed them me
      To kindle my cold love.

Dear, beauteous death! the jewel of the just,
    Shining nowhere but in the dark;
What mysteries do lie beyond thy dust,
      Could man outlook that mark?

He that hath found some fledged bird's nest may know
    At first sight, if the bird be flown;
But what fair well or grove he sings in now,
      That is to him unknown.

And yet, as angels in some brighter dreams
    Call to the soul when man doth sleep:
So some strange thoughts transcend our wonted themes,
      And into glory peep.

If a star were confined into a tomb
    Her captive flames must needs burn there;
But when the hand that locked her up gives room,
      She'll shine through all the sphere.

O Father of eternal life, and all
    Created glories under thee!
Resume thy spirit from this world of thrall
      Into true liberty.

Either disperse these mists, which blot and fill
    My perspective (still) as they pass,
Or else remove me hence unto that hill
      Where I shall need no glass.

HENRY VAUGHAN

The Hunting of the Hare

Betwixt two ridges of ploughed land lay Wat,
Pressing his body close to earth lay squat.
His nose upon his two forefeet close lies,
Glaring obliquely with his great grey eyes.
His head he always sets against the wind:
If turn his tail, his hairs blow up behind,
Which he too cold will grow; but he is wise,
And keeps his coat still down, so warm he lies.
Thus resting all the day, till sun doth set,
Then riseth up, his relief for to get,
Walking about until the sun doth rise;
Then back returns, down in his form he lies.
At last poor Wat was found, as he there lay,
By huntsmen with their dogs which came that way.
Seeing, gets up, and fast begins to run,
Hoping some ways the cruel dogs to shun.
But they by nature have so quick a scent
That by their nose they trace what way he went;
And with their deep, wide mouths set forth a cry
Which answered was by echoes in the sky.
Then Wat was struck with terror and with fear,
Thinks every shadow still the dogs they were;
And running out some distance from the noise
To hide himself, his thoughts he new employs.
Under a clod of earth in sandpit wide,
Poor Wat sat close, hoping himself to hide.
There long he had not sat but straight his ears
The winding horns and crying dogs he hears:
Starting with fear up leaps, then doth he run,
And with such speed, the ground scarce treads upon.
Into a great thick wood he straightway gets,
Where underneath a broken bough he sits;
At every leaf that with the wind did shake
Did bring such terror, made his heart to ache.
That place he left; to champian plains he went,
Winding about, for to deceive their scent,
And while they snuffling were, to find his track,
Poor Wat, being weary, his swift pace did slack.

94

On his two hinder legs for ease did sit:
His forefeet rubbed his face from dust and sweat.
Licking his feet, he wiped his ears so clean
That none could tell that Wat had hunted been.
But casting round about his fair great eyes,
The hounds in full career he near him spies;
To Wat it was so terrible a sight,
Fear gave him wings, and made his body light.
Though weary was before, by running long,
Yet now his breath he never felt more strong.
Like those that dying are, think health returns,
When 'tis but a faint blast which life out burns.
For spirits seek to guard the heart about,
Striving with death; but death doth quench them out.
Thus they so fast came on, with such loud cries,
That he no hopes hath left, nor help espies.
With that the winds did pity poor Wat's case,
And with their breath the scent blew from the place.
Then every nose is busily employed,
And every nostril is set open wide;
And every head doth seek a several way
To find what grass or track the scent on lay.
Thus quick industry, that is not slack,
Is like to witchery, brings lost things back.
For though the wind had tied the scent up close,
A busy dog thrust in his snuffling nose,
And drew it out, with it did foremost run;
Then horns blew loud, for the rest to follow on.
The great slow hounds, their throats did set a base,
The fleet swift hounds as tenors next in place;
The little beagles they a treble sing,
And through the air their voice a round did ring;
Which made a consort as they ran along:
If they but words could speak, might sing a song:
The horns kept time, the hunters shout for joy,
And valiant seem, poor Wat for to destroy.
Spurring their horses to a full career,
Swim rivers deep, leap ditches without fear;
Endanger life and limbs, so fast will ride,
Only to see how patiently Wat died.
For why, the dogs so near his heels did get

That they their sharp teeth in his breech did set.
Then tumbling down, did fall with weeping eyes,
Gives up his ghost, and thus poor Wat he dies.
Men hooping loud such acclamations make
As if the devil they did prisoner take,
When they do but a shiftless creature kill,
To hunt, there needs no valiant soldier's skill.
But man doth think that excercise and toil,
To keep their health, is best, which makes most spoil;
Thinking that food and nourishment so good,
And appetite, that feeds on flesh and blood.
When they do lions, wolves, bears, tigers see
To kill poor sheep, straight say, they cruel be;
But for themselves all creatures think too few,
For luxury, wish God would make them new.
As if that God made creatures for man's meat,
And gave them life and sense, for man to eat;
Or else for sport, or recreation's sake
Destroy those lives that God saw good to make;
Making their stomachs graves, which full they fill
With murthered bodies that in sport they kill.
Yet man doth think himself so gentle, mild,
When of all creatures he's most cruel wild;
And is so proud, thinks only he shall live,
That God a godlike nature did him give,
And that all creatures for his sake alone
Was made for him to tyrannize upon.

MARGARET CAVENDISH, DUCHESS OF NEWCASTLE

Sweet Suffolk Owl

Sweet Suffolk owl, so trimly dight
With feathers like a lady bright,
Thou singest alone, sitting by night,
Te whit, te whoo, te whit, te whit.
Thy note, that forth so freely rolls,
With shrill command the mouse controls,
And sings a dirge for dying souls,
Te whit, te whoo, te whit, te whit.

THOMAS VAUTOR

Thomas the Rhymer

True Thomas lay on Huntlie bank;
    A ferlie he spied wi' his e'e;
And there he saw a ladye bright
    Come riding down by the Eildon Tree.

Her skirt was o' the grass-green silk,
    Her mantle o' the velvet fyne;
At ilka tett o' her horse's mane
    Hung fifty siller bells and nine.

True Thomas he pu'd aff his cap,
    And louted low down on his knee:
'Hail to thee, Mary, Queen of Heaven!
    For thy peer on earth could never be.'

'O no, O no, Thomas,' she said,
    'That name does not belang to me;
I'm but the Queen o' fair Elfland,
    That am hither come to visit thee.

'Harp and carp, Thomas,' she said;
    'Harp and carp along wi' me;
And if ye dare to kiss my lips,
    Sure of your bodie I will be.'

'Betide me weal, betide me woe,
    That weird shall never daunten me.'
Syne he has kiss'd her rosy lips,
    All underneath the Eildon Tree.

'Now ye maun go wi' me,' she said,
    'True Thomas, ye maun go wi' me;
And ye maun serve me seven years,
    Thro' weal or woe as may chance to be.'

She's mounted on her milk-white steed,
    She's ta'en true Thomas up behind;
And aye, whene'er her bridle rang,
    The steed gaed swifter than the wind.

O they rade on, and farther on,
    The steed gaed swifter than the wind;

Until they reach'd a desert wide,
    And living land was left behind.

'Light down, light down now, true Thomas,
    And lean your head upon my knee;
Abide ye there a little space,
    And I will show you ferlies three.

'O see ye not yon narrow road,
    So thick beset wi' thorns and briers?
That is the Path of Righteousness,
    Though after it but few inquires.

'And see ye not yon braid, braid road,
    That lies across the lily leven?
That is the Path of Wickedness,
    Though some call it the Road to Heaven.

'And see ye not yon bonny road
    That winds about the fernie brae?
That is the Road to fair Elfland,
    Where thou and I this night maun gae.

'But, Thomas, ye sall haud your tongue,
    Whatever ye may hear or see;
For speak ye word in Elflyn-land,
    Ye'll ne'er win back to your ain countrie.'

O they rade on, and farther on,
    And they waded rivers abune the knee;
And they saw neither sun nor moon,
    But they heard the roaring of the sea.

It was mirk, mirk night, there was nae starlight,
    They waded thro' red blude to the knee;
For a' the blude that's shed on the earth
    Rins through the springs o' that countrie.

Syne they came to a garden green,
    And she pu'd an apple frae a tree:
'Take this for thy wages, true Thomas;
    It will give thee the tongue that can never lee.'

'My tongue is mine ain,' True Thomas said;
    'A gudely gift you wad gie to me!

I neither dought to buy nor sell
  At fair or tryst where I might be.

'I dought neither speak to prince or peer,
  Nor ask of grace from fair ladye!' –
'Now haud thy peace,' the lady said,
  'For as I say, so must it be.'

He has gotten a coat of the even cloth,
  And a pair of shoes of the velvet green;
And till seven years were gane and past,
  True Thomas on earth was never seen.

ANON.

The True Christmas

So stick up *ivy* and the *bays*,
And then restore the *heathen* ways.
Green will remind you of the spring,
Though this great day denies the thing,
And mortifies the earth and all
But your wild *revels*, and loose *hall*.
Could you wear *flowers*, and *roses* strow
Blushing upon your breasts' *warm snow*,
That very *dress* your lightness will
Rebuke, and wither at the ill.
The brightness of this day we owe
Not unto *music, masque* nor *show*:
Nor gallant *furniture*, nor *plate*;
But to the *manger's* mean estate.
His *life* while here, as well as *birth*,
Was but a check to *pomp* and *mirth*;
And all man's *greatness* you may see
Condemned by his *humility*.
    Then leave your open *house* and *noise*,
To welcome him with *holy joys*,
And the poor *shepherd's* watchfulness:
Whom *light* and *hymns* from Heaven did bless.
What you *abound* with, cast abroad
To those that *want*, and ease your load.
Who empties thus, will bring more in;
But riot is both *loss* and *sin*.

Dress finely what comes not in sight,
And then you keep your *Christmas* right.

HENRY VAUGHAN

News

News from a foreign country came,
As if my treasures and my joys lay there;
So much it did my heart inflame,
'Twas wont to call my soul into mine ear;
Which thither went to meet
Th' approaching sweet,
And on the threshold stood
To entertain the secret good;
It hover'd there
As if 'twould leave mine ear,
And was so eager to embrace
Th' expected tidings, as they came,
That it could change its dwelling place
To meet the voice of fame.

As if new tidings were the things
Which did comprise my wished unknown treasure,
Or else did bear them on their wings,
With so much joy they came, with so much pleasure,
My soul stood at the gate
To recreate
Itself with bliss, and woo
Its speedier approach; a fuller view
It fain would take,
Yet journeys back would make
Unto my heart, as if 'twould fain
Go out to meet, yet stay within,
Fitting a place to entertain
And bring the tidings in.

What sacred instinct did inspire
My soul in childhood with an hope so strong?
What secret force mov'd my desire
T' expect my joys beyond the seas, so young?
Felicity I knew

Was out of view;
And being left alone,
I thought all happiness was gone
From earth: for this
I long'd for absent bliss,
Deeming that sure beyond the seas,
Or else in something near at hand
Which I knew not, since nought did please
I knew, my bliss did stand.

But little did the infant dream
That all the treasures of the world were by,
And that himself was so the cream
And crown of all which round about did lie.
Yet thus it was! The gem,
The diadem,
The ring enclosing all
That stood upon this earthen ball;
The heavenly eye,
Much wider than the sky,
Wherein they all included were;
The love, the soul, that was the king
Made to possess them, did appear
A very little thing.

THOMAS TRAHERNE

A Song of a Young Lady: to her Ancient Lover

Ancient person, for whom I
All the flattering youth defy,
Long be it ere thou grow old,
Aching, shaking, crazy cold;
But still continue as thou art,
Ancient person of my heart.

On thy withered lips and dry,
Which like barren furrows lie,
Brooding kisses I will pour,
Shall thy youthful heat restore.
Such kind showers in autumn fall,
And a second spring recall;

Nor from thee will ever part,
Ancient person of my heart.

Thy nobler part, which but to name
In our sex would be counted shame,
By age's frozen grasp possessed,
From his ice shall be released,
And, soothed by my reviving hand,
In former warmth and vigour stand.
All a lover's wish can reach,
For thy joy my love shall teach;

And for thy pleasure shall improve
All that art can add to love.
Yet still I love thee without art,
Ancient person of my heart.

JOHN WILMOT, EARL OF ROCHESTER

Antiquary

If, in his study, he hath so much care
To hang all old strange things, let his wife beware.

JOHN DONNE

Song

Love a woman? you're an ass!
    'Tis a most insipid passion
To choose out for your happiness
    The silliest part of God's creation.

Let the porter and the groom,
    Things designed for dirty slaves,
Drudge in fair Aurelia's womb
    To get supplies for age and graves.

Farewell, woman! I intend
    Henceforth every night to sit
With my lewd, well-natured friend,
    Drinking to engender wit.

Then give me health, wealth, mirth, and wine,
  And, if busy love entrenches,
There's a sweet, soft page of mine
  Does the trick worth forty wenches.

JOHN WILMOT, EARL OF ROCHESTER

Song

Sylvia the fair, in the bloom of fifteen,
Felt an innocent warmth, as she lay on the green;
She had heard of a pleasure, and something she guest
By the towzing & tumbling & touching her Breast;
She saw the men eager, but was at a loss,
What they meant by their sighing, & kissing so close;
      By their praying and whining
      And clasping and twining,
      And panting and wishing,
      And sighing and kissing
      And sighing and kissing so close.

Ah she cry'd, ah for a languishing Maid
In a Country of Christians to die without aid!
Not a Whig, or a Tory, or Trimmer at least,
Or a Protestant Parson, or Catholick Priest,
To instruct a young Virgin, that is at a loss
What they meant by their sighing, & kissing so close!
      By their praying and whining
      And clasping and twining,
      And panting and wishing,
      And sighing and kissing
      And sighing and kissing so close.

Cupid in Shape of a Swayn did appear,
He saw the sad wound, and in pity drew near,
Then show'd her his Arrow, and bid her not fear,
For the pain was no more than a Maiden may bear;
When the balm was infus'd she was not at a loss,
What they meant by their sighing & kissing so close;
      By their praying and whining,

And clasping and twining,
And panting and wishing,
And sighing and kissing,
And sighing and kissing so close.

JOHN DRYDEN

To My Book

It will be looked for, book, when some but see
Thy title, *Epigrams*, and named of me,
Thou should'st be bold, licentious, full of gall,
Wormwood, and sulphur, sharp, and toothed withal;
Become a petulant thing, hurl ink, and wit,
As madmen stones: not caring whom they hit.
Deceive their malice, who could wish it so.
And by thy wiser temper, let men know
Thou art not covetous of least self-fame,
Made from the hazard of another's shame:
Much less with lewd, profane, and beastly phrase,
To catch the world's loose laughter, or vain gaze.
He that departs with his own honesty
For vulgar praise, doth it too dearly buy.

BEN JONSON

Song

Can life be a blessing,
Or worth the possessing,
Can life be a blessing if love were away?
Ah no! though our love all night keep us waking,
And though he torment us with cares all the day,
Yet he sweetens, he sweetens our pains in the taking;
There's an hour at the last, there's an hour to repay.

In every possessing,
The ravishing blessing,
In every possessing the fruit of our pain,
Poor lovers forget long ages of anguish,

Whate'er they have suffered and done to obtain;
'Tis a pleasure, a pleasure to sigh and to languish,
When we hope, when we hope to be happy again.

JOHN DRYDEN